The Family Tree

an illustrated novel

MARGO GLANTZ
translated by Susan Bassnett

SERPENT'S
TAIL

British Library Cataloguing in Publication Data
Glantz, Margo
   The family tree.
   I. Title
   863

   ISBN 1-85242-182-7

PB/23

RO16164 56 51

First published 1981 as *Las genealogías*. Copyright © 1981, 1986 by
Margo Glantz

Cover illustration: Frida Kahlo, *My Grandparents, My Parents, and I
(Family Tree)*. (1936). Oil and tempera on metal panel. Collection, The
Museum of Modern Art, New York. Gift of Alan Roos, M.D. and
B. Mathieu Roos. Photograph © 1990 The Museum of Modern Art,
New York.

This edition first published 1991 by
Serpent's Tail, 4 Blackstock Mews, London N4

Translation copyright © 1991 by Serpent's Tail

Typeset in 10/12pt Medieval Roman by
AKM Associates (UK) Ltd, London

Printed on acid-free paper by
Nørhaven A/S, Viborg, Denmark

Contents

A family engagement, 1950

To my family

The family in Mexico, with my parents on the left

Prologue

All of us, no matter whether noble or not, have our own family trees. I can trace mine back to Genesis, not as a matter of pride but because that must have been our starting point. My parents were born in a Jewish Ukraine very different from the Ukraine of today and even more different from that Mexico where I was born, where I had the good fortune to come into the world amid the shouting of tradesmen in the Merced market. My mother, dressed in white from head to foot, used to stand watching those same tradesmen in amazement.

I can't be accused like Isaac Babel of being precocious or bookish, since unlike him (or my father) I never studied Hebrew or the Bible or the Talmud (because I wasn't born in Russia and I'm not a male), yet I often find myself thinking like Jeremiah or avoiding the calling of the whale, like Jonah. I hear voices, like Joan of Arc, but I'm not a maid and I have no desire at all to be burned at the stake, though I am attracted to the gaudy (yet beautiful) colours that Shklovsky condemned Babel for when they were still young, and that he now hankers after nostalgically (Shklovsky, that is, because Babel died in a concentration camp in Siberia on 14 March 1941).

Perhaps what attracts me about my Jewish past and present is an awareness of its vividness, its colour and its grotesqueness, the same awareness that makes real Jews a minor race with a major sense of humour, with their ordinary cruelty, their unfortunate tenderness and their occasional shamelessness. I am fascinated by old photographs of a Lithuanian pedlar with his goatee beard (that invited persecution), wearing an outsize overcoat and smiling rather drunkenly at the camera as he offers his trinkets. By his side, looking serious and shabby, is the

1

vendor of dead men's clothes, the farmyard jackal who could smell out the imminent death of the man whose suit he would shortly be buying. I also feel drawn to those children at the *heder* (Jewish school) walking beside their grandfather, the boy with no shoes and the old man with his tired expression and white beard. But I don't belong to them, except for one distant part of me, the part which is closest to my father, a little peasant boy, the youngest of a family of immigrants, whose elder sister, Rojl, disappeared from the house when she was young, perhaps in Bessarabia (but perhaps somewhere else — what does it matter after all these years?) and whose brothers began to emigrate to the United States after the pogroms of 1905.

When I see a Warsaw shoemaker or a Wolonin tailor, or a water carrier or a Dnieper boatman, they look to me like my father's brothers, although his brothers became prosperous tradesmen in Philadelphia and swapped their skull caps and beards for clothes from the big department stores, probably Macy's. When I see Lublin children who can hardly reach the table and sit wearing their caps as always, in amazement, with some old books in front of them, while the *melamed* (teacher) uses a pointer to teach them the Hebrew characters, I seem to be seeing, through them, my father finishing his work in the fields, with his muddy shoes (on the other side of the Atlantic his brothers are wearing fashionable shoes), unable to play because he has to learn the ten commandments, Leviticus, the Talmud and the rules of those festivals and celebrations which are so alien to me.

I didn't have a religious upbringing. My mother didn't separate the plates from the pans, and made no clear division between containers that were for meat and those that were for dairy products. My mother, unlike my grandmother, never wore a wig to hide her hair because only the husband should see the hair of his lawfully wedded wife — and my grandmother Sheine was my grandfather's second wife (the first wife died — maybe in childbirth? No one knows, no one remembers). Their daughter Rojl, who vanished into the immense heart of White Russia, was the child of that first marriage. In compensation, I do remember the beautiful *jales* that were sold in the bakery, the proud Hebrew letters on those plaited loaves which have become established in Mexican baking now, since an uncle of mine introduced them into Mexico City before his assistant, Mr Filler, commercialized them through supermarkets. I never saw my mother taking her pot of *cholnt*, a stew made of tripe, meat, potatoes and beans, to the bakery (either of the ones belonging to my two uncles) to put in the oven on Friday before dark so that it would still be warm for mid-day Saturday and we could have a hot dinner without breaking the Sabbath, but I do remember my uncle Mendel praying by the window with his *tales* and his *vaymelke* but without any sideburns, swaying to the sound of his prayers as though he were shaking with laughter. In fact, it was really me that shook with laughter in the long hour before we sat down at the table, just as my two daughters shake with laughter when some member of the family sings the prayers before Passover or the prayers that sanctify Friday . . .

I have been in the bread ovens too. On the street called Uruguay, in that district where the streets are named after other South American countries, a reminder of the many possible futures that lay before us when we were choosing from all the unknown places where to emigrate. My uncle Guidale used to let us go inside the oven, still warm from Saturday, from which those little biscuits with quince hearts emerged, the ones that I could nibble at forever, because my uncle knew that my teeth were as tender as those of the mice that leave money in exchange for the milk-teeth of good children. Those little biscuits used to alternate with beautifully braided chocolate rings, whose hardness contrasted with the soft sweetness of the jam cased in exquisite pastry. I always dreamt of having a bakery and selling cakes and pastries; every time I gave a customer his bag full of wonders I used to look out of the

3

corner of my eye at some of the biscuits that were displayed in the windows, carefully arranged to entice gentile or Jewish customers into the shop. Beside the bakery was (and still is) *El Danubio*, but I didn't like seafood then.

One more thing: my mother tells me how, when my father's brother Albert died of cancer in Philadelphia, the only will he left was a piece of paper assuring all heirs that cancer is not hereditary.

I also see, from a long way off, a picture of my uncle Guidale with his guts and veins pulled taut, mourning his wife, my aunt Jane, father's sister, lying stretched out on the ground wrapped in a very thin sheet. She died after having cancer for a very long time, and his tears and his words were so moving, as were also my secret outings with a boy I was going with when Aunt Mira was dying of cancer of the liver, looking as cadaverous and yellow as the Jews in any concentration camp, and whom I saw little of before she died because I preferred to play truant with my *goy* boyfriend.

At home I have a few Jewish things that I have inherited — a *shofar*, a ram's horn trumpet, almost mythical, to proclaim the collapse of walls; a candlestick for nine candles that is used to commemorate another falling of walls during the Maccabee rebellion that José Emilio Pacheco, a *goy* like me, has sung of in Mexico. I also have an old candlestick from Jerusalem that my mother lent me and that has stayed here, but the candlestick stands beside some popular saints, some replicas of prehispanic idols (the man who sold them to me told me they were originals, but my friend Luis Prieto looked at them, licked his finger, ran it over them and said they were not), some altarpieces, some *ex votos*, and monsters from Michoacan, including a Passion with Christ and devils. Because of these things and because I put up a Christmas tree, my brother-in-law says I don't seem Jewish, because Jews, like our first cousins the Arabs, hate images. So everything is mine and yet it isn't, and I look Jewish and I don't and that is why I am writing this — my family history, the story of my own family tree.

1

I turn on my tape-recorder to start an historic recording; at least, it seems historic to me and a few friends. It might help to make some memories more permanent. My mother offers me blintzes with cream (she makes a lot of cream cheese these days, now she doesn't have the restaurant to look after, and my father makes 'interesting' poetry). I ask him about his childhood, and Jacob Glantz answers:

'I played, I ate a lot, and I looked at girls' behinds. I was very behind myself.'

'What age were you then?'

'Average.'

I go on asking questions, and ask the usual one:

'What did your father do?'

'He used to look after the cows, the horses and our fields and produce children.'

'How many children did he have?'

'I think he only used to go on having them because you couldn't get helpers in those days, you had to do everything yourself with your own two hands. We were five boys and four girls.'

My father came from a region of the Ukrainian steppes ('We had strong legs in those days, from going up and down so many steppes,' my father points out), where farming districts for Jews had been set up near a tributary of the Don, the river the cossacks sing songs to (along with the Volga), songs that my father used to sing when I was a girl.

My mother, however, lived in Odessa and her father imported 'exotic' things — tangerines, oranges, lemons, peanuts, pumice stone, possibly dark wine from Chios, tobacco (from Virginia?) and blue stone ('I don't know what that was for') and lots of other things.

'Where did those things come from?'

'Italy, Cyprus — the peanuts came from Singapore. What country is Singapore in?'

'What country? Thighland!' laughs my father, interrupting and we all fall about laughing with him.

Noise of cutlery on the plate of blintzes, spoons tinkle against the crystal glasses in their silver glassholders as my father puts five teaspoonsful of sugar in his tea and I seize the chance to insist: 'And where else did he import things from?' 'There was sesame seed,' says my mother, 'from Turkey. I don't remember, I wasn't very interested in all that. I was ten years old like your Renata is now, it was before the war, I hardly paid any attention. I do remember one tragedy though — a boat arrived with a big cargo of oranges from Italy and they'd all gone rotten, so they had to be thrown into the sea and all the fish got orange juice.'

'But that was in Odessa, and you told me that when you were very small you didn't live there, you lived out in the country a long way from the city.'

'My mother's parents were suppliers to sugar mills in Grushka, sugarbeet mills.'

'What do you mean, did they produce the sugarbeet and then sell it to the mills or what?'

'My great-grandparents and my grandparents rented out beet fields and then they bought up the harvest and sold it to the owners of the mills. They also had cattle and provided the villagers with meat and wool. They rented out the river too.'

'Rented out the river?'

I was used to hearing about land being rented out, but I'd never heard of a river being rented before.

'There were carp in that river and my grandparents used to sell them to the peasants.'

Fishermen and businessmen at the same time. My father

Father Mexicanised, 1935

knew all about it and says:

'Your mother's parents used to sell herring.'

Mother says nothing for a while, then says: 'They were freshwater carp.'

The taste of carp, the flavour of witticisms, all blend with the sweetness of strawberry jam stirred into the boiling hot tea.

'How did your parents meet?'

'Both my grandparents had beet plantations and they arranged the marriage. It was a meeting of two mills.'

My mother's parents emigrated to the city because the Czar forbade Jews to live off the land. My father's parents lived in a little farming community because the Czar did allow Jews from other regions to live by farming. Both those branches of my family were there at the same time . . .

2

Geography has never been my strong point. I have always mixed up northern rivers with southern rivers, particularly those that start in the Americas, and I confuse the fact that though my mother is called Elizabeth Mikailovna Shapiro and my father Jacob Osherovitch Glantz, in private their friends call them Lucia and Nucia or Yankl and Lucinka, sometimes even Yasha and Lucy, and in Russia they call them Ben Osher and Mama Liza. This fact (and having to get the right names for the right people, which hardly ever happens) has made me feel like a Dostoievsky character and made me realize something about the contradictions within me, that something special which is my Russian soul blended with the Mexican.

Yankl was brought up in Novy Vitebsk, in the southern Ukraine, in a village founded by a few survivors from Vitebsk, not far from Poland, when that country was torn apart and the Russians controlled the whole region. Czar

Alexander II granted land to the Jews provided they agreed to cultivate it, because the Ukrainian steppes were almost uninhabited except for nomads. My father's settlement comprised some three hundred or three hundred and fifty families, and once there were nine German families who taught them how to cultivate the land, in the middle of the last century, when my great-grandfather Motl came to that sparsely populated region and built the house that would later become my father's. Yankl confuses all kinds of things, he reverses incidents and alters images. He talks about the sense of humour and cheerfulness of his relatives which was well-known throughout the district, and only preserved in stories, such as the one about my great-grandfather Motl's intelligence, when he advised the members of the village who were asking for land to go for depth rather than breadth. My great-grandfather's village had been in Byelorussia.

'Byelorussia, yes, White Russia,' my father agrees, '*bielyi* means white. And there's also Malorossiia, Little Russia, the Ukraine, Lithuania, Latvia which were next door to each other, and Minsk, Kovno, Pinsk, Vilna etc. My mother came from Kremenchug, which was an important town in the Ukraine.'

I had known for only a few days where she came from, because amid my father's messy piles of papers, my mother had found a certificate belonging to my grandmother which stated the precise day of her birth, 17 May 1864, and the name of her native town. Today my father announces, to the amazement of my mother who had no idea, that he was born in Kremenchug too, and had left it when barely three weeks old. His brother Leibele, who died of smallpox at the age of three and who was younger than my father, was born in the village of Novy Vitebsk. Mother and I look at each other in surprise, and the doubt remains because the dates change every time he tries to remember. Never mind, the cloak of memory falls over writing, just as the sloping roof covered my father's house, the house with tiny windows, like 'little eyes with bushy eyebrows; the eyes were formed by the thatched roof, which was made of two pieces of wood shaped into a point, see? And there was straw up in the triangle where the two parts of the roof met, and when there were pogroms I used to hide up there. Underneath was the *kluniá*, the grainstore.'

In the distance and all around and as far as the eye could see was the great plain of the steppes. Those steppes so admired by Chekhov and Gogol, the steppes that inspired my father to write when Lilly, my elder sister was born:

The mountains of eternal snows are as strange to me
as the flat lands of Ukraine are strange to my child.

3

My mother's parents were born in a region full of beetroot, sugar refineries and rivers filled with sweet-water carp that never managed to reach the Volga. On the other hand, the Don cossacks had made trouble for my ancestors. My mother's parents' marriage was arranged by their families.

'We came from the Podolskaia Gubernia, as they say in the Podal state, a province of the Ukraine; my father was from Grushka and my mother from Ustia. The two grand-fathers used to supply the refineries with beetroot, because in those days they tried to make sure that a couple came from families in the same line of trade, they didn't want any workers' children. For the same reason, when I married your father, my father told me that he'd had to make sure that he wasn't the son of a shoemaker or a tailor, and I said: "Why should that matter?" and he said "You don't understand, that kind of man treats people badly." '

There is always poetic justice though. During the revolution, my mother's oldest brother, Ben Zion, actually did have to work as a shoemaker in a little village in the Ukraine that has since disappeared from the map.

It was agreed that the wedding should take place when both parties reached the age of fifteen, and they were married eighteen days after first meeting one another. My mother and all her seven brothers were born in that village, and she was the youngest but one. The youngest boy, Aliosha, died very young, fighting alongside the Bolsheviks. My grandparents left Podol when my mother was about eight, around 1910, because a new decree from the Czar forbade Jews in that area from working the land. My grandparents emigrated to Odessa, an important Jewish centre, and my grandfather Mikail was employed for a time in a canning factory belonging to some very rich uncles who later went to Moscow. Eventually he joined forces to set up an import-export business with one of my mother's cousins, Zalman Weisser, a foreign correspondent who knew several languages: Italian, French, English, German...

'Spanish, even?'

'No, you didn't need it much in those days.'

'What did they produce in the factory?'

'Sardines, I think there were tomatoes too, hundreds of cans. Odessa was a fishing port, there were all kinds of sardines.'

My grandparents lived at 21 Ievreskaia Ulitza, or Jews Street (and indeed it was full of Jews) and on the corner there was a large synagogue, while adjoining my grandparents' house was a well-known publishers, belonging to the great Ukrainian Jewish poet Bialik and his colleague Rovnitsky.

'There were trees all along that street, acacias and *seeren* which were big trees with little purple flowers, rather like the night-flowering jasmine in colour and shape. It was a lovely scented street. They hadn't put cement alongside the trees, just sharp little stones. I fell down once and I couldn't get up again because my knees were bleeding, and I cried and just then Bialik and Rovnitsky were passing by and they heard me and picked me up and took me back to my mother.'

11

'Who carried you, Bialik or Rovnitsky?'

'I don't remember. My mother was really frightened. Bialik was quite famous by then. He was rather short, very nice, not handsome but pleasant-looking, and Rovnitsky was tall, thin and rather frail, he was quite old and always wore a straw hat. I can still remember that, just imagine . . . Bialik, Hayyim Nahman Bialik, the Jewish national poet, who wrote about the pogrom of 1905, and about the first revolution which failed in his *In the City of Slaughter*. In that book he attacked the young Jews who had allowed the cossacks to rape girls and kill Jews. Though obviously if the young men hadn't gone into hiding, they'd have been killed too. His poem was translated into Russian and into other languages. A protest poem. The mother of my sister-in-law Sara was killed in that pogrom, she was at home sitting in her wheelchair because she was paralyzed and the cossacks came and started ransacking everything, and everybody heard them and hid because they were young and strong, but the old lady couldn't move and they killed her just for that. The cossacks were useful for national protection.'

'What?'

'The Czar gave them whatever made them happy. Especially after a revolt like the one in 1905. What was there to take in Jewish villages except the Sabbath candlesticks?'

'They weren't Jews,' said my father quickly, 'they were Pharisees.'

4

To understand what my paternal grandfather looked like and how his mind worked, all you need do is read Bashevis Singer. For though his life passed by just as it ought to, with children being born and work in the fields and religious ceremonies, every so often on special occasions he used to fall into a philosophical trance. His was a very simple philosophy, almost Confucian.

My grandfather Osher was 'a bit on the short side, I'd say,' good-looking with blue eyes. My grandmother Sheine, with her dark eyes, was as beautiful as her name. Her hair was completely hidden, because she wore a wig in the presence of everyone except her husband, but it was dark, because when she died 'just about seventy-eight years old', she did not have a single grey hair. She was good looking too, and very small. My maternal grandparents were more or less the same as my paternal ones, except that my grandfather Mikail was very tall and the colour of my grandfather Osher's beard was red-gold, just like my nephew Ariel. In effect, he looked like one of Babel's characters, 'a simple man without a trace of nastiness,' and though all redheads were thought to be violent, bad-tempered men, Osher Glantz was not, perhaps because the very light hair on his head made him not really a redhead.

In my father's house the food they ate was the typical food of Russian peasants. They carefully kept meat apart from milk, and because of this my father always says that Jewish babies at the breast are not truly kosher, because they very wisely mix the two. These strictly religious eating habits meant that when my grandfather came to Mexico he could not stay at my parents' house because their food was impure.

'Do you remember your father?'

'He was a good man.'

'Anything else?'

'He was poor.'

'Right, anything else?'

'He was poor. He had two horses, a pony or a colt, two cows, a little calf, some thirty chickens, a cockerel, a house with a thatched roof and an earth floor and a door with a notice on it that said "Push".'

'In Yiddish?'

'In Yiddish.'

'Anything else?'

'What else?'

'Well . . . Why do you say he was poor when he had so many animals?'

'It was a different sort of poverty, a very simple life if you compare it with the way people live here.'

'Did you have quilts stuffed with feathers?'

'Yes, my parents' bed was enormous and piled high with goose feather pillows. The front door opened into a big room where there was a table and chairs, and on the right hand side there was the stove and my mother used to sit on the floor sewing. Then further in there was another room, with another big bed which belonged to my parents. Then there were two little rooms off to the side for the boys, with very high beds and lots of feather pillows and there was a newborn calf in the house too, and when it was born it leaped about just like a colt. One horse was yellow and the other one was white. I wonder why I'm telling you all this nonsense!'

(Suddenly a feeling of nostalgia sweeps through me, nostalgia for those feather beds which my mother brought with her as her dowry for Mexico and which we used to leap on and roll around in on Sunday mornings, playing with father who used to cut our toenails afterwards.)

'Did he have a sense of humour?'

'Who, father? Once, when the peasants were arguing with the representatives from an agricultural organization (the Prikaz) to try and get more land, he said: "Don't fight, if they won't give you much by way of width, ask for it in depth, and that should do." I was twelve years old during the last few months of his life. I remember when he went to the village and I wanted to go too and he wouldn't let me, so I followed him for more than a kilometre.'

'Did he take you in the end?'

'Yes, in the wagon, which was a cart with four wheels and wooden planks and sacks full of corn that my father was taking home from the fields to give to the chickens. Before that he'd been to the mill.'

'What for?'

'To have it ground. Didn't you know that you have to grind wheat to turn it into flour?'

'Who did the mill belong to?'

'The wind and the village.'

'What was your father going to the village for?'

'He was buying things for the house, food. It was a holiday, the horses were tossing their heads and father was giving them wheat. Father was always very shrewd, in between one sowing time and another when he didn't have anything to do in the fields, he would go to the village and put new glass in windows.'

'What did your brothers do?'

'Mira and Jane lived with me a long time. My brother Moishe Itzjok went to the United States later on with my brother Abreml (Albert). They all worked in the fields too. Abraham was in the Czar's army for three and a half years. My elder brothers Ellis, Meier and Leie have been in the United States, in Philadelphia, since 1906. The younger ones went a few months after my father's death in 1915.'

'Why didn't you go too?'

'My mother couldn't go, she had her house, her team of oxen, her cart — she couldn't have left them behind. When my brothers left, Mira and Jane worked in the fields, especially Mira who was the strongest and the most responsible. Because I was little I went to the *heder*.'

'The *heder*?'

'Yes, Jewish school. We all went there from the age of three, and we learned the order of prayers, and the Hebrew alphabet. When I was thirteen, the year father died, we read the Talmud. After that, if we were good enough we could go on and study at the Yeshiba, the Hebrew university, but I had to go down the coal mines to help my family. There was a *rebe* (a teacher) among the peasants, and he had about twenty boys in the *heder*. We used to sit round a big table and chant the Bible, and he used to sit there and go off to sleep and the boys stuck his beard to the table with glue and he pulled his skin off trying to get up again.'

5

You never swim in the same river twice, or never get out of your depth, or still waters run deep, could all be proverbs that have to do with certain types of bathing.

My father's grandfather, *Motl der gueler*, 'Yellow Manuel,' I call him, 'No,' says my mother correcting me, 'the redhead,' came from Vitebsk, near Poland, to a village near Odessa, Novy Vitebsk, founded by a decree of Czar Alexander II, 'a good czar,' the one who was later murdered by terrorists, one of whom was Vera Figner, who used to make bombs, despite having come from an important middle class family and who, just like my mother later on, wanted to study medicine in Russia in that antediluvian time of 1872, and was only able to achieve her ambition abroad, in Switzerland.

Motl the Redhead had seven sons, one of whom was my grandfather Osher, and another was Uncle Kalmen, murdered in a pogrom.

'The settlement was divided into two parts, there was a river that ran through the middle and right on the edge were the public baths.'

'Weren't there any baths in the houses?'

'No. The men used to go and have their baths there on Fridays.'

'What did the women do?'

'The women had the *mikveh*, and when a woman's period ended, she went to the *mikveh* and made herself kosher again for her husband.'

My father's school was beside the public baths. In the daytime the boys helped in the fields and in the evenings they studied and round about nine o'clock they set off in the direction of their own homes and walked together past the public baths which, according to the *sheidem* legends, were inhabited by demons (the nasty kind). My father used to walk past hanging on to the teacher's hand and one night, while crossing the bridge that spanned the river, he saw something white in the darkness. Yankl was terrified and started to cry. He didn't want to move from the spot and the rabbi had to push him past the thing, which turned out to be a beautiful white horse with a long mane and a gentle disposition.

These images remain, they linger on, returning over and over and that white shape travels with the emigrants.

There were baths in the houses, or rather there were washbasins, but the public baths were there for proper bathing, for holidays and for the Sabbath. The caretaker of the men's baths was not a Jew, he was a *goy*, but the caretaker of the women's *mikveh*, the ritual pool, had to be Jewish. The *mujik* supervised the men while they bathed and gave them massages, he even used to enjoy beating them with teazles. It was a sort of Turkish bath with some features of a sauna.

Jews were not allowed to look after the baths. This seems like a remnant of the Talmudic prohibition that forbade Jews from becoming barbers, a prohibition that forced Samson into the hands of Delilah. Moreover, according to the Talmud, it is an unworthy profession to be a barber and no father may teach it to his sons. According to the *Midrashim*, the Talmudic commentaries, the evil Haman, who tyrannized the Jews and was punished thanks to Queen Esther (from which comes the feast of the Purim), practised as a barber for more than twenty years. Of course I am very proud of my hair, because on my father's side there were redheads and King David was supposed to have had red hair too. Apparently my mother was never very keen on the colour of hair in my father's family, because when my sister Lilly, the eldest one of our Mexican dynasty, was born, the first question she asked was not whether it was a boy or a girl but:

'Does it have red hair?'

'No, it's a blonde girl,' (the midwife would have answered).

The bathing attendant for women was Jewish naturally, she used to cut their nails and make them step seven times into a tub and then into a large, quite deep bath, with several steps down so that they could get right under the water. The bath was called the place of purification and the bathing attendant decided when a woman was finally pure and kosher.

'The *mikveh* was like a well, there was always running water.'

Once my parents start talking they embellish, and the seven times that the women conceal themselves, submerge themselves and cover their heads to purify their flow of blood becomes forty-nine.

'What do Jewish women do for baths in Mexico?'

'Some of them go to the *mikveh*, some don't.'

'Your sister Lilly went to one before she got married.'

An experience that I have never shared with her, because my marriage(s) were outside the tribe.

The Jews were set apart from neighbouring peoples in Biblical times, among other things on account of their bathing practices and because of the way they cut their hair. The women had to keep their hair hidden. Who knows whether the excessive sexual freedom of today isn't due to the fact that hair blows wildly in the wind and purification baths have gone out of fashion.

6

'When we were at high school, every morning we used to sing an anthem for the Czar and a religious hymn, because it was before the revolution then and it was a Jewish high

Mother and father in Mexico, 1925

school, you see.'

I look at her and she smiles; she is reliving it all. She remembers a girl, Lida Trilnik, a friend who was younger than her, who was in the kindergarten (my mother went to school in first grade) and who was dressed as a butterfly at a concert.

'Then I went to the conservatory and took classes in singing, solfa, harmony, and piano. What use have they been?'

Mother played the piano and often used to play a piece that has engraved itself for ever on my mind too. Its scales sound like an impromptu by Schubert, but it has a Russian flavour — I call it Cock-a-doodle-Dolokhov, an advanced but childish mixture of Tolstoy and the banal.

'Yes, before starting classes we used to sing, wishing the Czar good health, and then we said, "God save him because he is the most powerful emperor on earth, etc.," And then we would go on, "I thank God because he gave me my soul (God, not the Czar), I thank God because he woke me up, because he gave me my soul back when I woke up." When the war began we didn't sing any more, as a sign of national mourning. I think the headmistress used it as an excuse to cut down on expenses.'

At school, before the war, the headmistress wore a long dress with a train. She was a short woman with a corset that held in her waist and made her look like a wasp. The same woman suddenly appears at home, with her hair down, and wearing a day dress that covers her curves without obliterating them. Her empress's train rebels against ordinary everyday life, and the gloomy figure from school suddenly puts on its best party clothes, like the day when the headmistress marries off her daughter.

'She got married before the revolution. Her husband was a very famous violinist.'

A memory comes to mind here. It's a false memory, it belongs to Babel. I often have to turn to certain writers to be able to imagine what my parents remember. The passage mentions a certain Zagursky, who was noted for having 'a factory of child prodigies ... a factory of Jewish dwarfs with lace collars and little patent leather shoes ... The souls of these fragile creatures with swollen blue heads harboured a powerful harmony' (I think of the famous child prodigies, the violinists: Misha Ellman, Jascha Heifetz, Isaac Stern). Perhaps the husband of the daughter of the headmistress of mother's school studied with Zagursky.

'The girl was very beautiful. Blinder, her husband, was a famous violinist, and later the two of them went to California, where he played in the best orchestras. They got married in the Odessa synagogue where they had a choir, a great singer and a great rabbi. It was a reformist synagogue like the ones in Kiev and Berlin. The person who played the organ was Polish because there weren't any Russian Jews who could play in Odessa. It was a very special occasion, there was a choir with girls, which was very unusual because women couldn't sing in the temple. Very solemn, very beautiful. Jewish weddings could still be held in the synagogue, that was in 1918. Then they were forbidden. The bride looked like a doll, she was very tall. They went to the Crimea on their honeymoon; when they came back she was already filling out.'

There were three Jewish high schools in Odessa: the Zhabotinsky, the Kaufman Zak, and the Getzelt, where mother went.

'At the Zhabotinsky, they taught Hebrew and Russian, in mine they only taught Russian, and they didn't teach Yiddish in any of them. I learnt Yiddish in Mexico, and I never learnt Hebrew. There were other girls' schools in the capital, they were called after the Czarina, Marinskaya Gymnasia, where Jewish girls were not admitted. Only Jews from the wealthy upper classes were welcome there; for example, those who had mines in Siberia.'

'Mines in Siberia? — Didn't they just deport people there?'

'No, there were gold and silver mines, some people had furs and sold them, there was a lot of money around, you know. They were privileged Jews and could go to any school. I was in one for Jewish girls because at the time there weren't any mixed schools, they came with the revolution, and in those schools you studied for eight years to go to university and it was very difficult to get in, that's why the girls got so nervous and so gloomy, as if it were the eve of Yom Kippur, the Day of Forgiveness, a day of fasting. There was a panel of assessors who always made excuses. I experienced it once, though not trying to get to university, because as a matter of fact it didn't happen like that any more by then — the revolution had already taken place, you see. Well, as I was saying, I got a particularly nasty panel, a man who asked me how to take someone's pulse. I gave him a very complicated explanation which was no good at all, until the teacher at that school, who wasn't Jewish, pointed to his watch. That was how you took someone's pulse, with a watch.' (She pauses and then goes on.) 'Silly questions,

21

they were very nasty people who made all kinds of excuses so that we couldn't go to university. It'll be enough to tell you that a panel tried to stop a cousin of mine, before 1914, from graduating as a doctor. I was on a visit to his house, I was twelve at the time, and there was a group of undergraduates all very worried, wondering how they would pass the final exam if they didn't convert, because they wouldn't give degrees to Jews.'

'What happened in the end, did they get their degrees?'

'That was just when the First World War broke out, and my cousin was accepted as a military doctor. In wartime, everybody's useful.'

7

Bashevis Singer says somewhere: 'The Jews don't record their own history, they lack a sense of chronology. It is as though they knew instinctively that time and space are just an illusion.' This sense of elongated, gelatinous, compressed time that has a single theme with multiple variations and cadenzas resembles my parents' lives, where endlessly repeated conversations can suddenly shed a spark of light on some happening that ideal historical time has never satisfactorily explained. Time is a space marked out and filled with the ceaseless chanting of prayers by which a devout Jew measures his life.

And also his death. Then they have to say *kaddish*, blessing the holy name of God and remembering the departed, all seated on the ground without shoes so as to get nearer to the earth and accompany the one who has gone on ahead.

'I used to go to the synagogue next to the ritual bath-house to pray for my father. I was the only one who was able to pray for him in the place where he died. My brothers did it in Philadelphia.'

'What did you feel?'

'A great warmth because I was sitting next to the stove and the old men were praying all day long, chanting psalms and I felt less of an orphan there. First we read a chapter from the *mishnah*, the oral tradition, and then we said *kaddish*, praising God and remembering my father's name.'

'What do you say in *kaddish*?'

'At least ten Jews have to come together to make up what is called the *minien*, which is a congregation. That's the right number to hold whatever ceremony you want. "May his name be blessed forever and throughout eternity." That's what all poets hope for. There was a great poet who came from my village, about thirty or forty years older than me, Simeon Frog. Whatever happened to him, goodness knows. My brothers went to Philadelphia, I only remember the younger ones, Moishe Itzjok who didn't want to hand over three and a half years of his life to the Czar and emigrated along with Abreml who had just come out of the army where he'd served the full duration. In 1939 when I saw my elder brothers Meier, Ellis and Leie, it was like seeing them for the first time. Leie told me that when they left they accused him of having given me a false kiss.'

'Why was it false?'

'Because I didn't feel it.'

'Your grandmother,' says my mother, 'was marvellous. When she got to the United States she travelled from one end of the country to the other to see her sons and she didn't know one word of English. She had all sorts of things written down on paper and she taught them everything and crossed the four points of the compass to see them.'

'She loved your mother a lot,' says Nucia rather sadly.

'Yes, and I loved her too, she was a splendid woman, she never caused any trouble, she always tried to help and never interfered in a nasty way, always out of a desire to do good. Quite unlike a mother-in-law.'

My grandmother is very indistinct in my memory. She was in Mexico twice, first in 1928 before I was born and then from 1936 to 1939. She died there. She was very ill in the last months of her life, whilst in mine she barely fills a fleeting space, one marked by a photo in which I am in the foreground and she is in the countryside. She is also part of a legend that enhances my father's life: when she was already very ill, my grandmother Sheine (or Sofia, according to her passport) waited until her youngest son, who was visiting Philadelphia, came back to Mexico before departing this life. At that time we were living in the Street of the Argentine Republic, number 96, in a three-storey building with a courtyard where we used to play as children.

8

The new Jewish cemetery was near the hill of the Star. The old one was near the Burial Vault of Griefs. My father remembers another cemetery when he was thirteen years old, just after the death of my grandfather Osher. Nucia was working for a wealthy relative in a mill, helping to count the sacks of grain which the peasants brought in at night.

My father had to keep watch, but sometimes he would nod off to sleep, sitting next to the mill. The gentiles came and to wake him up they would pee noisily, sometimes down the slipway that fed the grain into the stone mill-wheels, from which Jacob had saved himself with a single leap. He was in the Ukraine, in a village called Krivoy Rog, about a hundred and fifty leagues from Novy Vitebsk, his native village; it was winter, and it was 1914 too, the year the war started.

One day he was going home in a *svostchik* (a small carriage) when he came to Sofievka, a Christian village with twelve or fifteen Jewish families and a burial vault. A great storm came up, an early spring blizzard. The coach driver and his horse found shelter in a stable, and my father went to see a relation, Eizel Jilbuj, who looked after the cemetery.

'I went to look for somewhere to spend the night. I knocked and knocked. Eizel was enormously tall, and used to stoop, and had a white, white beard. He came out carrying a lantern and angry and said to me:

"Yankl? What a surprise! Come on in."

'I went in feeling pretty frightened, because I knew it was a graveyard. In I went, the first thing I saw was this funeral bench where they strip and wash the dead bodies, with a little broom next to it. I felt a bit panicky and wanted to get out, but I couldn't, I had the night and the snow outside and dead bodies inside.'

Eizel woke up his old lady who put on the samovar and offered my father the customary glass of tea with a lot of sugar and then showed him where he could sleep, next to a window.

'I couldn't sleep. I lay down, all hunched up. I didn't know what to do. Then I shut my eyes tight and the old lady told me not to worry. I slept a bit, then all of a sudden there was a tall figure by my side, with a piece of rope and an axe in his hand calling me and I woke up. He was shouting and telling me we had to lasso the dead first and then he would cut their heads off with his axe. I shouted too, I yelled, and the old lady got up again.'

The old lady came in and restrained the crazy old man with his long white beard; then she told him off (I guess she was very small, they must have been one of those classic couples where the woman is really tiny and the man is huge, but the woman is the one who shouts loudest) and she woke him up and took him back to bed. She explained:

'Eizel has started walking in his sleep. Ever since they took Yerujem off to the war.'

Next day Eizel didn't remember anything about the night before. My father was still shaky, but his old relative offered him a splendid breakfast of bread and butter, herrings, semolina, tea and more tea, more bread and butter and jam; after that he took him out for a walk round the cemetery garden, showing him the paths and pointing out the children's graves, covered in flowers and almost buried in the snow, then he proudly pointed out the family mausoleums, he showed him how well laid out it all was and he said it all as though he were showing Adam round Paradise, a long time before the first sin and, obviously, a long time before the arrival of Eve.

Then he asked him if he would like to stay on for another night. My father replied hastily that he preferred to stay buried in the snow on the road home rather than spend another night among the dead.

It is seven leagues from Sofievka to Novy Vitebsk. In Sofievka there were just a very few Jews and a graveyard.

9

'Around 1915 or '16 they informed us that the Czar was coming, along with the Czarina and their only son, the Czarevitch, I think he was called Alexei. All the schools in Odessa had to march past, in their special uniforms, and because it was winter we always used to wear white pinafores with a little white cape and a hat, and in winter we had beaver skin (do you know what a beaver is?) and around our hats we had a narrow bright green ribbon with a bow in front.'

'Lime green or nile green?'

'Green, some sort of green, dark, rather nice, pretty green. What does that matter? Oh, Margo! But before the revolution we wore checked uniforms, in blue and black, or, I don't know, purple and lilac. And we had to wear a flower on our capes, I'm talking about the Czar's visit now. There was such a fuss trying to find gloves, because there were no gloves to be had in the city. My mother was tired out looking for gloves and that flower, I don't know if it was real or artificial, and shoes too, and because I was tall, even though I was only in the fourth or fifth year, they put me in with the seventh form because they wanted us all to be the same height, like rows of soldiers. I remember it all happened in a flash, there was an open carriage and horses, and we could just see the Czarina and her children, five of them, four girls and a boy. Czar Nicholas II, Czarina Alexandra Feodorovna, you always have to give the father's name too, Nikolai Nikolaievich, Alexandra Feodorovna and I was Elizabeta Mikailovna . . .' she laughs, and emphasizes the name, 'with the father's name, Nikolaievich, son of Nikolai, you couldn't manage without a father . . . and that was it, we spent so long getting ready for the great day and it went by so fast we almost missed it.'

'What do you know about Rasputin?'

'The son, the Czarevitch, was very sickly, like a lot of people in royal families who intermarry, the boy was a haemophiliac. Then he became very ill and the Czarina was always worrying about him and Rasputin was a blackmailer, he said he could cure the boy, and since he was always at court and had lots of privileges, because it was very important to save the boy, there was a lot of gossip about him, they said he was very close to the Czarina. You know, I've got one of those magazines that Tamara sent me from Russia where it says that during the revolution they were taken away from the royal palace and kept in a basement and the Czar asked them to save the Czarevitch's life, he was just a boy and the heir and very delicate. The Czar saved the people who later killed him, he pardoned them, Lenin's sister was caught and sent to Siberia, there weren't any executions then, they just sent them into exile, and the Czar pardoned her along with other revolutionaries, but they didn't want to pardon the Czarevitch and they shot them all, in one room, in a basement, but it wasn't Lenin's fault. Later on they all said that one of the daughters escaped, it might have been Anastasia. The Czar was a very weak man, very delicate, not aggressive like Ivan Grozni, you know who I mean, Johan Grozni, Ivan Grozni, they're the same man, Eisenstein made a film about him, he was a very cruel person who killed a lot of people, I think he was very evil. Prince Kurbski had talks with Johan Grozni, Ivan the Terrible, but that's another story.'

'Kurbski with a V or with a B?'

'Like I wrote it for you, with a B. You never could tell the difference between a V and a B, I always have trouble in Mexico because people can't tell the difference here between one letter and another and they can't understand you. Kurbski with a B.'

10

When grandfather Osher died, Yankl went to stay with his uncle Moishe Haim, an unqualified mining engineer.

'My uncle was a wealthy man, he used to work in the coal mines, which was where most of the money came from in Krivoy Rog. He was very modern, he'd shaved off his beard, not like my father who kept his long like the old style Jews did. Your mother's father was modern too, he had a little pointed beard that you could hardly see. Before he went to work in the mines, my uncle had mills and supplied the military with food. I was with my cousin Ilusha, who was much older than me, they were very nice to me, they treated me like a poor relation. My girl cousins, I remember them well, they were tall, handsome, strapping girls, who went to private school, because in my village the state school only had six grades and they only took Jews who spoke Russian.'

'Not Yiddish?'

'Not Yiddish, nor Ukrainian either. In Krivoy Rog there was a Jewish university, a *yeshiba*, and *gymnasium*, that's what we called a high school.'

'Not one city in the Ukraine,' says mother, 'had up to a million inhabitants. Odessa was really important, but there were only about four or five hundred thousand people living there. There were some other big cities, Kiev, Herzon,

Nikolaiev, ports on the Black Sea, and Krivoy Rog and Kremenchug where your grandmother Sheine was born.'

'She was a very intelligent woman, even though she was uneducated, she couldn't read or write Russian, only Yiddish, and not very well either, but she was very intelligent. They didn't educate women in those days, even though she was born in a city. You have to remember it was mid-way through the last century,' says my father.

'And what about the revolution. Where were you when the revolution happened?'

'That was a very interesting time in my life, the revolution caught up with me in Krivoy Rog. In 1915 I was in the village and in 1916 and '17 I was in the city with my uncle, though the revolution didn't reach the little places, only the deserters made it out there. They went from the villages to the city too, and then because everything was in turmoil a lot of people came to our village, begging, there was no food in the cities, but out in the villages there was never any shortage of food. All those people belonged to the intelligentsia. Then some Zionist Jews came through who set up a little *ajshara* in my village, they were training settlements for those who wanted to go to Israel. This *ajshara* went on to Constantinople later and when my mother and brothers went to Turkey in 1922 they saw them there again. They wanted to take them with them to Israel, but my mother preferred to go and join my brothers in the United States. They were very helpful to me, I read with them, I learned Russian well, and when the revolution reached our region I became a revolutionary.'

Mother has been washing the dishes in the kitchen, but now she comes in and tells us to go to the table because tea is ready. We sit down and my father carries on talking enthusiastically. Before this I have spent days trying to persuade him to tell me something about his youth and he has refused because it all seemed uninteresting. Suddenly something strikes him:

'Before 1917 there hadn't been any pogroms in our

villages, but everything came with the revolutionary movements. But I've told you all that.'

'I've just come across something really interesting,' says mother, 'I think you'll be absolutely fascinated.'

'Wait just a minute, mother, father's remembering things he's never told me about before. Let's hear what he has to say.'

'Do you want tea?'

'Yes.'

'The revolution. Sit down here, Margo, are you all right? The revolutionaries wanted to free the Ukraine, there were all sorts of groups, good, honest people who wanted to help and bands of bandits trying to kill us all. Oh, yes, I've certainly lived an interesting life! The world war, the revolution, what an experience! Since everything was upside down, people used to come and hide out in my village, some very well-educated, very intelligent people, who taught me a lot. I'll say they did! They made me into a revolutionary. They were young men and women too, they must have been about twenty-two or twenty-three years old.'

In 1921 he was in Herzon, where he took a course to become a teacher of Marxism, which he continued in Odessa in 1922.

'Once they sent me to Moscow as a delegate for the youth of Odessa at an agricultural congress, and I met Lunacharsky and Radek, the Bolsheviks. Lunacharsky had an aristocratic background, he came to attend the lectures on cattle shows and he brought an actress with him. Lunacharsky was an interesting man, he was tall like Radek. Do you know who Radek was? He came from Galicia.'

'From Poland? Was he Jewish?'

'Yes, he was a Polish Jew, but he was part of the Russian revolution. I think his name was Rosenfeld, he was one of Lenin's Bolsheviks, Karl Radek. I met Zinoviev and Kamenev too.'

'And Kalinin,' says mother.

'I saw Kalinin too, but what did I have to do with the likes of them? I was just a lad, I saw them from a distance, I was interested in what they had to say, but I was too insignificant to be with them. I met a lot of leaders at that time too. Kamenev and Zinoviev were both Jews.'

'Zinoviev was Trotsky's brother-in-law,' adds mother.

'I had a lot of diplomas and certificates dating from that time, but when I was going through the Polish Corridor at Danzig I went into the toilet on the train and tore up all my papers, I don't know why. I was frightened and I tore them all up and lost the lot.'

'Not all,' I say smugly. 'I've got some of them, they're all in bits.'

'Like our lives.'

11

My mother's (or was it my father's) rich relations emigrated to Moscow after the revolution and when my parents, Liza and Ben Osher, were on their way to Mexico, they went to see them and were not given a bed. They stayed in a house belonging to the young revolutionaries where there were collective dormitories.

'They were collective because the boys used to come in at night to see the girls and there were a lot of babies with collective fathers.'

This dramatic footnote of my father's reminds him of his adolescent passion for a wealthy neighbour with a large house, who had no father and a half-mad mother (he said she was mad because she got upset when my father used to go round on summer evenings and look at her daughter or caress her). The young woman was well-built and went to a school in a nearby village called Krivoy Rog — a god-forsaken place, like Cuernavaca. Uncle Moishe Haim lived there, the one my father talked about almost more than his own father. He had somehow become rich, which was obviously very rare in a poor, country family. His image takes on definite characteristics, he appears as an engineer (of sorts) in a coal mine, and as an impresario, though that image is blurred when I try to find out if he took in my father to look after him or just to make him work. Sometimes my father is a poor orphan child toiling away in a rich relation's mill, and at other times he is the poor friend of the family's youngest son, with whom he has long talks and his photograph taken.

Since all the recollections are mutual, the product of two people's minds, my mother Lucia remembers that she could not study much either, because during the revolution they began to impose quotas on anyone who was not a worker's child. Lucia studied chemistry at first, then she was forced to switch to medicine, but they didn't let her finish that either and she started on an odd career (here too memories and discussions get mixed up). Eventually I learn that my mother obtained her diploma as a medical assistant, a higher rank than that of nurse, in 1922.

'Do you still have your diploma?'

'Your sister Susana has one of them and the other was stolen by one of your father's lady friends.'

Such a friend that when she heard that my parents were emigrating to America she went off with the diploma and forged it by changing the photo. Not only that, but, according to my father, she also seduced my beloved uncle Volodia when he was still very young and naive. Lucia insists, because Volodia was her brother, Volodia or Vladimir:

'She was your friend.'

The family 'friend' made off with the diploma and with my uncle's virginity. This put an end to my mother's chances of working. Zina Rabinovich, that is, Zina the Rabbi's daughter, stole my mother's medical diploma which could have helped her find work in Mexico.

'Your mother was very good-looking, she couldn't ever

have worked, women didn't work in those days.'

Nevertheless, the director of the General Hospital invited my mother for an interview.

'Your mother was very good-looking, they used to steal women away in those days.'

'Just a minute, let me finish.'

The director general's house was new and very elegant, in the Roma quarter. At mealtimes such a large group of relatives gathered that you might have thought it was a tribal feast. My mother dressed in white from head to foot: white stockings, white shoes, white dress, white hat, in other words the outfit worn by a decent young Russian lady in hot weather.

'They must have thought I'd gone dressed for my first Communion.'

I think she went dressed as a nurse so that they would give her some work, but what they gave her was a green mango. (Can you imagine what it must have been like for pretty, young woman dressed all in white to eat a mango for the first time?)

Afterwards my mother found some private work, with a German doctor, Schmitbergen, and she stayed quite a while with him. She left that job because the doctor lived above his consulting rooms and his wife used to fight with him so violently that furniture was broken, and then they always had a reconciliation and my mother decided it was too much to handle.

Afterwards she was interviewed by a Jewish doctor from Chicago, Dr Border, who worked in the Lecumberri prison and helped abolish the death penalty. My mother went with him once to the great wall pitted with holes where they shot the prisoners, and the doctor explained simply that she couldn't possibly have the job because women 'just don't count.'

'There wasn't a single woman doctor anywhere in Mexico at that time. Dr Border had been in Chicago for many years, but he was born in Russia.'

33

My mother didn't know what had made him come to Mexico to help prisoners who were treated 'like animals' with absolute impunity. Besides providing them with medical care, Dr Border taught them a trade.

'I felt so useless not working,' said my mother gloomily.

12

'A tall cossack and a short one passed by our house, their hands covered in blood, and my mother, crying her eyes out, washed their hands in a bowl.' My father's mother wore broad skirts under which she hid my two aunts, Jane and Mira, girls of sixteen and seventeen.

'I was almost out of my mind, I walked (I was only a boy), I ran from one place to another and crossed the town over the little bridge that led to the baths and I tried to shelter in my uncle Kalmen's house, he was my father's brother. It was 1917, I went into my uncle's house and I almost went mad, my uncle had a long curly red beard, all crimson with blood, and he was sitting with the blood pouring down and his eyes open. The fear of death still hadn't left him, perhaps he was still breathing! Beside him, wrapped in a sheet were all the household utensils, everything made of silver or copper, the Sabbath candlesticks, the samovar. I was scared stiff, I had no idea what to do, I just ran out of the village like a madman. The pogrom lasted several days, I went out into the country and I found an abandoned well, deep, but with no water in it, and I spent several days in it. When I heard that everything had calmed down, I came out. Before that, I could hear the terrible cries of the girls and children.'

It all happened so fast that one pogrom followed another.

'In those troubled times different groups were chasing one another and as they went through towns and villages they laid waste to everything in their path.'

It all sounds so familiar, it's like those revolts that our

nineteenth-century novelists wrote about and like what you read in novels about the Mexican revolution, the revolts and the levies, the confusion, the sacking of towns and villages, the deaths.

'The Bolsheviks came back and we had some of the short rifles left by the bandits and some of the horses too; only those who'd been in the world war knew how to defend themselves, the rest of us were saved by a miracle. Many of the bandits were peasants who knew us, and they killed the people they stole from to make sure they couldn't be denounced.'

Yasha hid in the house of a *muzhik*, a friend of his grandfather's, Sasha Ribak. He had 'an enormous moustache, like the poet Sevshenko' (the great popular poet of the Ukraine). My father stayed hiding in a corncrib, breathing through a hole, even as bandits stuck their bayonets into it. Ribak took him food and water and let him out when things calmed down a little.

'General Budiony's Bolshevik cossacks arrived. When things were a bit calmer, I came out. When it was dangerous I went back into hiding again. I remember Sasha well, he was very good. I wrote a poem about all that, in 1920, in Russian.'

'And what about your mother and your sisters, how were they saved?'

'We survived by chance, by luck. My mother and my sisters hid in the top of the house, where there was a loft used as a storeroom, in the space under the rafters. As the groups were all chasing each other they hardly had time to look. They sacked and killed everything they found in their way. My mother was saved that first time because she washed the cossacks' hands.'

13

Sometimes they show documentary movies in the Regis

cinema and girls with dark curly hair file over and over again into a concentration camp, then sometimes quite deliberately they walk into crematorium ovens. Usually they look like me, and seeing those images has left me with a daily sense of guilt that clings, guilt at having escaped a number branded on my right wrist or the indelible mark of the yellow star that was sewn onto overcoats in Parisian winters. Even Max Jacob had to wear one when he went outdoors, despite the fact that he had converted to Christianity.

Someone interrupts my recollections and the guilt dissolves. It doesn't matter much whether you're a Jew or not, what matters is whether you're willing to fight against the herd instinct.

My father remembers the pogroms, my mother does not. Lucia only remembers the story of Ilusha, the brother who was to die during the Second World War through eating a potato when he was starving. Ilusha joined a group of other young students fighting bands of outlaws who were robbing and killing Jews in the villages. The group was counter-attacked by White Russians who beat them savagely and decimated them. Ilusha went home suffering from tuberculosis. He was already doomed.

'During the Civil War,' says Nucia, 'the partisans and the bandits were interchangeable, there were red ones, white ones, green ones who followed General Zeliony (that means green in Russian), or the *kolchakovets* who followed general Kolchak, he was a White Russian who commanded a cavalry regiment. Then there was Makhno, the trade union anarchist and his Jewish assistant, Voline, who were active in the Crimea and southern Ukraine. Makhno was a real anarchist, he used to gallop by with his horses pulling little carriages called *tachanki* and waving a black flag.'

His beliefs were clear enough, but when they passed through the little Jewish rural communities, his men ransacked everything, raped and murdered.

The groups may have been interchangeable and persecuted one another, and without exception, they all devastated the villages, those ten or twelve Jewish villages near the one where my father was (Zholta, Kuschinsk, Zlochistaia and the rest), organizing pogroms 'officially'.

In 1918/1919, some of the young men from my father's village decided to defend themselves and hoped to join the partisans in the village graveyard, building armed barricades among the graves.

'The bandits sent two or three spies to see if we had any defences, and they saw us and came back with some cavalrymen and killed all the defenders.'

'What happened to you?'

He smiles and says: 'I hid behind the graves with five or six others and we all got away. Besides, the bandits were being chased by another group led by General Grigoriev, he was an aristocrat and a counter-revolutionary, and he gave his cossacks the freedom to plunder and destroy every house they came to.'

Behind Grigoriev there was another group, Bolsheviks this time, who were following them to 'clean up the bandits in the village'. Some of the partisans were caught and shot by the river bank.

'Sometimes even the Bolsheviks killed us and ransacked the place, because it was chaos then. Later they imposed some sort of order, and when the Civil War ended, the pogroms stopped too.'

When peace was restored to the region, only thirty per cent of the inhabitants of those agricultural communities founded by the Czar for the Jews were left.

14

Having an ancestry and not having one are both relative. Lucia hands over to me some little scraps of paper, 'little scraps of life,' which contain her history, and diplomas are unrolled. It is the same with this black Rosencrantz piano, which must have been on earth for at least a hundred and fifty years and whose story is contained in the missing candelabra which have nevertheless left a mark on the wood. Now it is used by my nephew Ariel who plays jazz on its out-of-tune keys. The first time it was played after being acquired by the family was by Jacob Kostakowski, the composer, a friend of my parents, who had helped them choose it at the pawn shop. It cost 180 pesos. The scraps of paper are crumpled and on the reverse side there is the stamp of some old Czarist banking house. Later, during the revolution, the paper was used again and up in the top left-hand corner the name of the Socialist Republic of the Ukraine is printed. These are my mother's high school diplomas, where it states that she studied chemistry or music at the Conservatory; there are also some from the city of Herzon where my father was teaching literature. Others relate to a specific time: the last year in which the high school of Odessa existed, the year when my mother had to end her studies as medical assistant.

My parents argue a lot. My father takes advantage to tell a Jewish joke, in which an old Jew goes to the rabbi and asks him to grant a divorce from his wife because she is deaf. The rabbi says to him: 'But you can cure that, there are machines.' 'Yes,' says the husband, 'I bought her one, but when I talk to her she takes it off.' I remember snatches of conversation, but nothing complete, because the documents have fragmented it all.

My father lived in the town of Herzon. He left his native village when the pogroms became unbearable, or when he realized that he would not survive the next one. In Herzon he taught in a local school. He was a teacher of literature, and his boss was Mikail Mirsky, a writer and teacher who was well-known in Russia at that time. 'He was well known, he didn't have to be on the left or on the right, he just taught and was respected for it.'

My father could get enough food for his sisters and his

mother. He had his payok, that is his ration-book, and he also belonged to a North American society, the ARA, which sent books and food to Jews from abroad: bags of coffee and packets of chocolate which were distributed by the Jewish committee.

'I had all those things then. I had chocolate, but I couldn't get bread.' My father lived with his family in an old bath-house in the city suburbs, they had a little stove that only heated part of the house and worked with wood or coal.

'Outside there was so much starvation that when I arrived in the autumn of 1921 there were three hundred and fifty thousand inhabitants and when I left in the spring of 1922 there were only thirty five thousand. Ninety per cent of the population starved to death. During the bad winter when it was very cold the streets were full of starving people and there were rows of dead bodies piled up on top of each other three and four deep. Going down the street at night you'd hear people crying out "I'm hungry", "I'm dying", but we couldn't help them. When the snow melted the great epidemic started and the streets stank.'

Along with the chocolate my father received bacon and shoes 'with pointed toes', also buckwheat and condensed milk. Sometimes the peasants from the surrounding countryside came in, bringing foodstuffs and little round rolls that people fought desperately to get hold of.

15

My grandmother and two aunts were given permission to leave Russia in 1923 to rejoin their family in *America, America* (as Elia Kazan's autobiographical film has it). My father was doing his military service and had to stay in the Soviet Union.

'Your mother was afraid that I'd get lost in the revolution. I was very impulsive, it was a dangerous situation and the revolution didn't tolerate people who were impulsive. What the revolution demanded was total obedience from each individual, and anyone who tried to see things their own way was put on the list of counter-revolutionaries. Well, I was pretty well done for, as you can imagine, being a loud-mouthed Jew. Later on they arrested me.'

'Why did they arrest you?'

'They arrested me for . . . you see, I was marked down in the revolution as a man with nationalist deviationist tendencies.'

My grandmother and my aunts stayed on in Russia for another year after being granted permission to leave, because my grandmother was afraid she might never see her son again. But in the end they travelled to Turkey and then they couldn't go any further, because the North Americans had restricted their immigration quotas and only their mother was eligible to enter the United States. However, my father was also granted permission to leave, though afterwards he went to a meeting that had been called to protest about unfair discrimination against people looking for work. One of the men who had been refused work threw himself out the window in protest, then the police arrived and put most of the protesters in jail, including my father.

At this point in the story a friend of the family turns up, a pro-Soviet Jew who had left Russia around 1924 and emigrated to Cuba in 1928, from where he had been chased out by Machado's henchmen because of his militancy. He has brought some Soviet journals sent him from New York, at the enormous cost of 123.50 pesos.

'They used to reach me quickly direct from Moscow. They only cost 17.50 that way, but you have to pay a full year's subscription.'

'When did you leave Russia?'

'My family left first. My father went to the United States in 1912. He left my mother in Russia with the children. In 1914 he sent us tickets and we were due to leave on the 19th of August and the War broke out on the 29th. My father went back to Russia in 1922, but he couldn't settle. He was a businessman and they accused him of being a bourgeois, so in 1923 he went to New York with his two brothers. I went to Cuba in 1924, but then they brought in new regulations about immigration quotas so I couldn't go on to the United States.'

'That's what happened to us too,' says Yankl.

'I went on to Mexico later, because otherwise I'd have ended up drowned in the bay of Havana.'

His friend leaves, and my father comments:

'You know, he's one of the very few who's remained left-wing.'

He insists on recalling that meeting where a worker threw himself from the window. I remember something similar in one of Wajda's films.

'Then the riot started,' interrupts mother. 'The police were there and they started taking workers away. They took your father along with a friend of his, a journalist who was about forty. Your father didn't return and I was worried and I started looking for him round the police stations. I asked different policemen about him and nobody knew anything. I said to one of them, you've got your people all over the place, don't you know or can't you tell me? He told me he couldn't say anything. It was a Thursday. On Saturday a lady came to see me. I was playing the piano and she asked me if I was Glantz's fiancée. I was surprised, but I said yes. I've brought you a message from your fiancé that my husband gave me when I visited him in prison.'

16

We have always complained about our Jewish Christian heritage and our tendency to masochism and all the moaning that comes with it. As a contrast, I like Isaac Babel, that friend of my father's 'of middling height, with glasses so thick that when he used to read his eyes went right into the pages.'

They went right through, and his voice recounted dark comic tales, sometimes tinged with fresh blood, or dressed up in feathers, like the story about Odessa. 'My Pigeon-loft,' which my father heard him tell before it was ever published, at a meeting of the Russian Writer's Association that had been founded after the revolution.

'Babel used to live in Moldavanka, a run-down district of Odessa on the outskirts of the city, in Griboyedowskaia Street. He was a poor Jew, whose father was a tailor, and knew Yiddish very well, though he wrote in Russian. His writing was sharp and to the point, and he wrote what you might call sketches, rather like Chekhov's. I used to get money from my brothers in the United States, and several poets would come and see me at home, when I lived in Politzevkaia Street, number 22 (which was the street where the police had their headquarters during the time of the Czar). They changed its name after the revolution and called it Kondratinko Street, after a hero in the Red Army. Brodsky used to come, and Babel, though none of us ever thought he'd become so famous, and we used to drink vodka in a cellar.'

The glasses bore through the paper again, and Babel reads his story about a young Jew lying naked in the gutter, after the pogrom, with his curly, blond pubic hair exposed, and all the girls gathered round to admire him. My father laughs and remembers how all the members of the Writers' Association laughed when they listened to Babel, even when Babel told how he and Kozma the street-cleaner found his grandfather Shoil lying in the street all bruised and battered after the cossacks had been through and how Kozma trimmed his beard for him.

'A lot of writers belonged to that Association: Osip Osipovitch was one of the older ones, he used to edit a magazine for children called Kolosia. Kolosia means when an ear of corn is growing and inside it there's a seed and the wind bends it over as if it were praying (and I seem to see my uncle Mendel when he recites the psalms). I was very young in those days and a free-thinking anarchist. I used to go to all the public meetings, including the protest meetings and once we were all protesting when Trotsky came through Odessa, on his way to exile in the Crimea. I remember him before that, when he came with Lenin, with his *dziniel*, the great big cloak just like Gogol describes it, pulled up round his ears and all the people were shouting: "Long live Lenin and Trotsky, *Vozhdi narodna*, leaders of the people." Trotsky was quite young then, he had a moustache and was a marvellous speaker.'

'What else can you remember about Odessa?'

'Oh, I can remember a lot about Odessa, everything. Just ask me, and I'll tell you. Your mother didn't know any of this, because she was middle class and I used to take her all over the place. There was another friend of mine, what was his name? I had one called Niezna Kome, nobody's ever heard of him, he was daft, he stammered and he wasn't a poet, though he did write, he even wrote sketches. He lived in Odessa too and belonged to our group.'

'What about Nabokov?'

'I never met him in Russia, he was a lousy poet, I met him in Switzerland in 1948 or '49. I always liked mixing with writers, and he had a Jewish wife who translated his work. She translated him into English, then afterwards he wrote in English, but he always thought in Russian. He was a White Russian, he was one of the first ones to go abroad in 1918. He talked a lot and then his tongue ran away with him like a dog.'

My friend Annunziata remarks: 'And with good reason too, since he wrote such filth.' I am reminded of one of Pavlov's dogs.

'Did you talk much to him?'

'I never met him personally, I just met him as part of a group at a conference.'

'Later those early Ukrainian writers founded another

writers' group called *Potoki Oktobria* "Rough water", because some water flows sluggishly and some flows rapidly, there's a nice poetical word for it: now what would it be?'

I leave him trying to find words that sound poetical, with his glasses firmly in place.

17

'Yes, they used to come round every morning to leave things they'd written for me to read. That went on for ages, I was about eighteen or nineteen then, it's more than sixty years ago now since Babel wrote *Red Cavalry*. He wasn't a red, though he was a writer who Gorky admired. They killed Babel later on, the swine! He came from a poor family, a really poor family. Years just sink into eternity, you have to go right down deep into the past, like diving into water, and that's eternity. Writing is a great thing, I believe writing is greater than painting, it's more expressive. Anyone who can do both is really fortunate! It's like having two heads, like kings do. Now here comes your mother, the queen. What do kings have on their heads? A crown.'

I listen and I see things too. I see the great Diego Rivera in his painter's smock or dressed like a Russian workman, arm in arm with Maria Felix, the beautiful actress. I have seen them both before, on her balcony near the President's palace. Later, I meet them with my parents in the foyer of the Bellas Artes building; I'm thirteen years old. They've just finished playing Brahms Third Symphony and a woman who is completely carried away by it all says: 'Chavez played brilliantly and I adore the Third'. The Great Actress in her glittering dress and her jewels doesn't even deign to look at her, she merely says loftily: 'So pleased to meet you.' I see her again in one of her films, when Jorge Negrete is carrying her in his arms, and I enjoy a good cry, just like that time in the cinema when I went to see Marie Antoinette (Norma Shearer) with my big sister Lilly and cried. I cried so hard that people were shouting at us to leave the cinema. Lilly was more angry than the rest of the audience and we weren't able to stay to see how Norma Shearer had her head cut off, though I don't think they did cut off heads in films in those days.

Lilly can remember Ruth Rivera, the painter's daughter, who was at school with her in Secundaria 3, the most famous high school at that time, the time when revolutionaries used to buy Cadillacs. Lilly says that Ruth was very tall, 'she was the tallest of the lot, and the only one with hair in plaits, she used to take on all the teachers, and was a really turbulent character, though Diego adored her.'

'She was with Diego all the time,' says my brother-in-law Abel Eisenberg cryptically.

'Yes,' my mother interrupts, 'about fifty years ago we were neighbours in Acapulco when Diego was living with Lupe Marin. I don't know if she remembers me, she was very tall and well-built and older than I was. Is she still alive? Diego used to say hello to us in Russian, he spoke it very well, very precisely, with a foreign accent, but very well. We saw him at the Bellas Artes with Frida Kahlo, she was wearing a purple or lilac shawl, he was painting her and he said to us in Russian: "I just can't get the colour right no matter what I do." Frida was lying down.'

Perhaps it was draughty.

Characters stream by and one inspects them like the king in Lope de Vega's play *La Estrella de Sevilla*, when he marched through the city and looked at all the girls leaning over the balconies.

A few days ago I met Lupe Marin; before then I had only ever seen her portrait. She is still very tall, though slightly bent now. She talks about Diego and her eyes light up, they were always such good friends, she assures me, though they were only married for seven years. At the beginning they used to talk about Diego's marriage to Frida 'because she

Wedded uncles, on my mother's (left) and father's sides

treated my daughters very badly and that made me very
angry. Diego was ruined by women and the Communist
Party. When he died, he didn't have any money in the bank,
just seven thousand pesos and the doctor was charging a
thousand pesos a day. I offered him one of the paintings he
had given me and he said he wouldn't dream of taking it.'

Nowadays Lupe won't touch salt and only eats fruit,
apples, oranges, and peaches, like those Dutch painters who
painted dazzling still lifes, or like Cézanne. Luis García
Guerrero listens to us, knowing for certain that he can
produce better fruit than the real thing. He even paints
peach stones, but never touches watermelons or radishes.

'What about grapes? Have you painted them?'

'Never.'

'Because they're too small', says Lupe.

18

'Lida Trilnik.'

'Start the tape and listen,' mother orders. 'The first time I met her was when she came to high school, she was in one class and I was in another. Before the war there used to be one great big playroom, and in one corner where there weren't any windows a little group of girls was practising for something, probably for a party, I don't know what. I've always remembered her because she was a butterfly, she was such a pretty girl.'

'Really lovely, she was. Do you remember her, Margo? So good-looking. More or less the same age as your mother, wasn't she?'

'No. She was a year younger. I remember what she said to the butterfly hunter: "Be good and don't touch me. My life is so short, it only lasts a day." Just think how old she is now.'

'Oh, come on.' says father.

'Ein minut', says mother impatiently, 'let me finish. We used to study together.'

'She was two years younger than you and her maiden name was Shotjin. You know what that means, Margo?'

'Yes, a matchmaker.'

'She left school in the fifth grade and after that I lost touch with her. It was such a great shock to run into her in Guatemala Street in 1926. "What are you doing here?" she said, and I said "What are you doing here?" and it was such a shock. I was with my husband and she was with hers, and so we didn't meet up with them.'

'She used to come to the restaurant quite a lot,' says father, 'but she came on her own. We didn't meet her husband.'

'Then all of a sudden one day in 1960 she telephoned me and said she was going back to Russia because she'd heard that her younger brother, her only brother, was still alive. She had been told by the Maderos, then the ambassadors to Moscow. "Aren't you ashamed of yourself?" she said to me.

"Why don't you go back to Russia and look up your brothers? Both Benia and Salomon send you their best wishes." '

Lida Trilnik's brother fought in the Second World War and was awarded the Red Star for bravery.

'Like many others, his parents didn't manage to get out of Odessa and they took all the Jews to a place called Kulekovoye Polie (it was a famous place before the revolution, that's how I remember the name), about as big as a parade ground with barbed wire all round it; they took all the Jews, men, women, children, old people and poured petrol on them and burned them alive.'

'Who did? The Germans?'

'No, they say the Romanians did it.'

'Yes, they burned them all alive,' father repeats.

'I don't know who it was,' says mother nearly in tears, 'I don't know. There were thousands of people there who saw it, and they didn't do anything or say anything. Lida's brother just couldn't talk about it.'

'What does her brother do? Is he still alive?'

'Yes, he is. He was younger than Lida.'

When she went back Lida revisited her parent's house, number 10 Deribasovskaia Street.

'That was the most aristocratic street I can remember before the revolution. It was paved with wooden tiles, it was so unusual. There were only a few horse-drawn carriages around in those days. They were called phaetons.'

'I remember that too,' adds father.

'She went to this house and knocked on the door. A big man with a white beard came out, and she said. "I've come from overseas, my parents used to live here, would you mind if I came in and had a look round? I grew up in this house." The man invited her in, and then after showing her round the house they sat down at the table and he said to her: "Where have you come from?" She said she came from Mexico, and he said he had a sister there, and then my name was mentioned and it was just like a film, one of those amazing coincidences and they were both so taken aback they cried. She told me all that in 1960 and I talked to her again yesterday to check up on the dates you were asking me about, Margo, and we went over it again. Isn't that amazing? We run into each other in Guatemala Street and then she meets my brother in Odessa in the same house where she used to live with her own family. Isn't it fantastic? Of course they were living there because her parents were dead and when my brother came back to the city he had nowhere to go, because sixty thousand houses had been destroyed.'

We pause for a minute. Mother serves noodle soup, we eat and relax and then she brings in fried veal with beetroot salad and for dessert there is strudl, served with very hot tea.

'Afterwards she got to know my brother Salomon and they all became very good friends. Whenever Lida went to Russia she always used to go and visit him.'

'What did your brother do?'

'He was a Soviet civil servant. He was a very special person, she liked him a lot.'

19

'My brother Salomon was surprised to learn that his sister ran a restaurant. The last thing he imagined was that I could have had anything to do with something like that. Once he went to see Lida Trilnik while she was in Odessa and he brought her a little cake and asked her: "Do they make cakes like that in my sister's restaurant?" Lida didn't know how to tell him that we made the best cakes in Mexico at the Carmel. (Croissants, coffee cakes, napoleons, date cakes, chocolate cakes, beigels with lox and vanilla cream, pastry shells with jam and strawberries and thousands of other varieties were all piled high on the Carmel's tables.)

'What a pity,' says mother, as she drinks her tea and I

choke on my home-made strudl, 'that none of my brothers is still alive. Misha used to live in Kiev, that's where he got married, he had a wife and two children, both grown up. We never knew them, and both his sons died in the Second World War. He and his wife died in Babi Yar, that's all I know. He was my third brother.'

'Was your mother still alive then?'

'Yes. She and my other two brothers, Salomon and Benia, the two older ones, were evacuated with their families to Alma Ata beyond the Urals, and that's how they came to survive.'

'What happened in Babi Yar?'

'Don't you know? Seventy thousand Jews were buried alive in a communal pit. The Nazis killed them.'

'It's not the first time such a thing has happened, and it won't be the last,' says father. 'I translated Yevtushenko's poem into Spanish.' He recites the poem half in Russian. 'I am afraid, I feel as ancient as the Jewish people, as though I were myself a Jew.' 'Yes, the Nazis issued an extermination order: "All Jews must present themselves with their belongings and hot food in the street behind the graveyard. Anyone who does not arrive by 7 a.m. will be shot."'

'What about your brother Ilusha?' I ask my mother.

'My fourth brother lived in Leningrad. He lost his only son in the war, he was a pilot.'

'Did your mother write and tell you that?'

'No, my brother Salomon did. During the war the whole family was separated and people were moving around all over the country either because of their work or because it was safer. Ilusha was on his way somewhere when the Nazis took Leningrad and he just happened to meet Salomon at a station. They wanted to see each other and write more often, but a few days later Ilusha died because of the blockade and the starvation, his intestines collapsed, it was 1945. He left one daughter, who was twenty-six then and my brother Salomon wrote to her saying he considered her the same as his own daughter. Our family was very close.

Ilusha's wife is still alive, she was always very sickly, she had tuberculosis, but, God be praised, she's eighty-two or eighty-three now. Salomon's daughters both married, one married a captain and the other married a Soviet army colonel. My brother wrote to me and said, "of course they're both Jewish." He told me that because in the Czar's days there weren't any high-ranking Jewish officers.'

'Salomon's dead now, isn't he?'

'Yes, he was the last one, Benia died before him. My niece Lilly lives at 89 Karla Marx Street (that's how you say it in Russian) which used to be Ekaterinierskaia, named after a Czarina. She lived there after she got married in 1919.'

'What's my cousin's name?'

'I don't know, but she lives in apartment 3. She's a pianist and I don't know how many children she has. She was always very delicate. Benia had three sons, the second one was called Grisha, he wrote to me a few years ago: "I'm little Grisha, I was one and a half when you went away, now I'm sixty." They had two sons. My mother was alarmed when she heard I had four daughters. She was delighted when Lilly was born, and when you were born too, but she was a bit alarmed when Susana arrived and she couldn't believe it when I had Shulamis.'

'But she had seven children.'

'She never saw two of them again, one died in the revolution and two died in the war. Now there aren't any left at all, not even uncle Volodia.'

'Did you send her photos of us?'

'Of course I did, with all of you dressed up specially. I was very careful about that and I even used to have special clothes made for you all, by the mother of Dr Boalostoski, you know, the heart specialist. I had a sewing machine that I paid 15 pesos for, which worked the opposite way to the pedal ones. I made ... well, I made all sorts of things, baby clothes, cushions ... everything that came to hand. That machine was a godsend, I don't know where I bought it nor where it disappeared to. Why aren't you eating, Margo? You

MARGO GLANTZ

haven't eaten a thing.'

(Not a thing, except ripe fruit, steak, kasha, noodles, mashed potato, fruit salad, cakes, strudls and then, eventually, tea and more strudls. My mother thinks I'm looking very thin.)

20

In a book that came out recently in France, Karl Marx's daughters describe in a series of letters how their chances of happiness were destroyed by having the famous man as a father. When one of them, Eleanor, was born, Marx told his faithful Engels: 'Unfortunately, it is one of the particular sex.' Marx can perhaps be forgiven if one thinks that one of his sons had already died and the other was dying, and that his only male offspring to survive was the son he had by a servant, the son whom Engels as a true, devoted friend, adopted as his own so as to keep things quiet, which none of Marx's daughters knew about until the death of their father's bearded companion. Marx's daughters were taught all the skills proper to girls, such as piano lessons, riding lessons, readings from Engels and Carlyle and correcting the proofs of *Das Kapital*.

But obviously Marx is only part of my story. I mentioned him because my parents didn't have any sons either, and perhaps my father might feel less afflicted knowing he stands in such illustrious company.

As for sons, I don't want to impute anything to anyone.

Curiously enough, my mother was the only daughter in a house where only sons were born.

'Your mother's family was utterly bourgeois. Your mother used to play the piano.'

When my father met her, Lucia was going out with a tall, blond, handsome boy, 'very middle class,' whilst my father was a revolutionary.

'So why did you become such a reactionary?'

'It's not me that's reactionary, it's the rest of them that have turned into anti-revolutionaries.'

My father was received at my mother's house thanks to some relatives, though they were not at all sympathetic to him, because they imagined, quite rightly, that this outsider was trying to run away with the one member of the family belonging to the particular sex.

Nucia for his part complains about getting involved with the middle classes:

'The girls I used to mix with wore boots, and had long hair and were tough. Your mother was interested in fashion, she used to wear gloves and dainty little shoes and my friends used to say they didn't know where I'd picked her up, she looked like something out of a museum.'

'Your father was a revolutionary, and he used to come to my house up the left hand staircase, the service stairs. He had long hair, like a hippy before they were invented.'

Since Nucia is a poet, our conversation runs the risk of sounding like Neruda's songs of desperation or something ultra-modernist (youth, divine treasure etc.).

The feelings of nostalgia are very strong. I'm only sorry that I have no way of recording what my parents looked like when they were talking.

'I came from a completely different environment. The years I spent during the revolution were the most interesting ones, the most important years in Russian life, from 1917 to 1925. The proletariat in those days believed in social revolution, they made reforms, they believed in the future, it was a time of great idealism when people thought the quality of human life could improve, they believed society could be changed, people didn't just live for themselves, and this is true, they lived for others as well. But then traitors started to rise to the top . . .'

My father goes on: 'Trotsky said that Stalin would be the one to destroy the revolution, he'd be its "son of a bitch". In

Hebrew, "son of a bitch" also means "grave-digger".'

21

'I just don't understand your father, he always has to pass himself off as a victim.'

'Weren't you ever happy with mother?'

'Always.'

But he goes on complaining. I suppose it's second nature now.

'I was very happy with her. I wouldn't have been who I am without her, because I've got a mind that wanders and she's got a good sense of direction.' (Laughter, a lot of emotion, a few hurried sips of tea, sounds of teaspoons on glass: the glasses nestle in silver glass-holders that are a reminder of the old Russia.)

Nucia admits that he was always very casual about life.

'I was never very responsible. It was thanks to her that the family stayed afloat, not just because she worked but because she always protected us and kept us ship-shape.'

Now I perceive my mother as a great Russian *mamatshka*, like those dolls that you can open to reveal lots of smaller, even more authentic ones. And my father, with his wild, curly, uncombed hair is suddenly transformed into a somewhat damp young Moses, rocked by the waters of a rather stagnant River Nile.

I shuffle the possibilities, both concrete and abstract, like the good Party man Georg Lukàcs, as to what my family history might have been if my mother had stayed in Russia. Or if my father had. What would have happened if Lucia had married that nice man Mari, the 'serious' one? Maybe I'd have been a dental surgeon or a barrister in a wig with the heavy muscles of someone who only eats butter and strawberry jam.

Maybe we'd have died in a German bombardment or

My parents on their 50th wedding anniversary

overloaded our stomachs from eating too much food after the long periods of hunger during the Second World War.

At least my father has managed to stay married for fifty-six years, nearly fifty-seven now, and here I murmur super-stitiously the holy words against the evil eye, *Kainenore*.

I remember the day when we were celebrating my parents' fortieth wedding anniversary. We went back to Carmel, the restaurant we used to own, and waiting at a table was Pedro Coronel, the painter, surrounded by empty beer bottles that served both as his halo and as a screen.

When he sees my father come in, he says indignantly:

'Where've you been, Jacob? I've been waiting for you.'

'I've been celebrating a wedding anniversary. I've been married forty years.'

'You mean you kept me waiting for something as daft as that, you old Jewish son of a bitch.'

Coronel uses the Spanish word *cabron*. Coronel's *cabron* has associations of classical imagery, of the bearded billy goat, an image that bears a dangerous resemblance to

Trotsky, known as Lev Davidovich Bronstein, who said when he met my father in Mexico:

'You look just like my brother.'

And maybe that brother kept his old Hebrew name, and maybe along with it the recurrent heritage of tradition.

22

I always wanted to be Flash Gordon. Yes, ever since I was a little girl, and I never wanted to be Dale Carter nor even Ornella Muti as the vicious Aura. I would have liked to fly through the skies on a rocket cycle, in black and white just like Flash Gordon in the serials of my childhood. In fact, I once travelled with KLM when it used to take twenty-eight hours (at least) to get to Amsterdam, and you got off the plane with swollen feet and twenty-four hour jet lag (at least) and you went to the cinema the night you arrived and saw *The Wages of Fear* with Yves Montand and you went to sleep in the bends in the road where they killed the hero in an over theatrical way. Later, you went round the obligatory museums and asked for van Gogh or Vermeer and nobody knew anything about them and then you thought that the Dutch were really ignorant and uncultured, until you discovered that The Hague was Den Hah and that Fan Hoh was the painter who cut off his ear.

Then on to Brazil, and you landed in Rio, the most fantastic city in the world with its Sugarloaf Rock and its Christ at Corcovado, its orange trees and the Lolitas of Ipanema, and above all, the black magic that stretches right the way up to Bahia. The first thing I look for has nothing to do with writers, the reason why I undertook this whole journey (to Cuba, Nicaragua, Costa Rica, Venezuela, Peru and Colombia). Instead I go looking for the magic laces of the Señor de Bon Fim which bring good luck, and have one fastened round my left wrist, coloured violet, white or orange. I also look for a charm to go round my neck and I start asking everyone where I can find one. The novelist Manuel Puig looks at me disillusioned; he doesn't believe in witchcraft, but a psychoanalyst friend of his uses a lace of The Lord of Good Death in therapy sessions and holds ceremonies for tying it on. You have to be open to the world, relaxed and completely honest, you make three wishes and each time you think about anything really important you have to close your eyes and feel the knot in the lace and then look out towards death. All the taxis in Rio have a good supply of laces, and when we go to see the Minister of Education to try and set up an exchange between writers I'm still wearing the shameful cord round my wrist. Feeling rather guilty, I cross my arms and put my free hand over the thing (as though I was taking my own pulse). The Minister looks askance at me, and his secretary, a stunning Brazilian woman dressed all in red and with hair dyed like Jean Harlow's is also wearing a similar sign on her wrist. I stammer and forget what I'm there for. Elena Urrutia, my travelling companion, is not wearing one and she knots the thread that I left hanging and when we leave (after seeing the Candido Portinari frescoes), I heave a sigh and fall into a drowsiness that stays with me until evening when we go out to dinner with Nelida Piñon, the writer and a good friend of mine, who takes us to a restaurant along Copacabana. I tell her my story. She looks at me the way the Minister had looked and then she opens her handbag and takes out several laces. Then she takes hold of Elena's arm, asks her to uncross it, ties on a fabulous lace and actually gives her three more as a present. Next morning we are visited by another psychoanalyst who has lived at Bahia and who brings us another three laces (very brightly coloured, that's the least I can say about them) and wishes us the best of luck. We accept the gift and fly on to São Paulo, where we hope to meet a Holy Mother, a friend of Martha's (the second psychoanalyst) who, I hope, will purify me. Afterwards we meet Vera de Cunha Bueno, cousin of a federal member of Parliament who also looks at our range of coloured laces with distrust. She says loftily 'Superstition!' and takes us off to the city museum of Catholic religious art.

Back in Mexico my father looks contemptuously at the famous laces which my daughters are all wearing on their left wrists, one violet and the other pink. When I go round for supper at my parents' house my mother looks and doesn't say anything, she serves us soup with matze meal balls, turns and looks at me again, and when she goes out to the kitchen I seize the opportunity and try to hide the lace with my watchstrap. My father sees what I'm doing and asks:

'What is it, the filthy object?'

Renata shows him hers and says:

'It's one of my mother's supersitions, Lord knows where she got the idea from.'

23

'I've never read so much in my life,' says my father, 'I've read three books since yesterday, they're really great. Have you read them? The sons of Abraham, we're all sons, that's for certain . . What? you want to fly on the thirteenth? No. Margo, you don't ever go anywhere on the thirteenth, you travel on the twelfth or the fourteenth. I forbid you to go anywhere on the thirteenth.'

'Where did you get that idea from?'

'Nowhere. My mother taught it me. You never travel on the thirteenth.'

I have a lovely period photo, sepia coloured, with all the characters in a row, and their gentle trusting faces, photograph faces that nobody ever looks at now. They are the *shif brider*, the ship brothers, because besides blood brothers you can have all sorts of other kinds of brother and these are ship brothers. The photo was taken in Amsterdam, they're all on their way to America, all Jews, some from Poland and some from Russia, and there's a goy, a non-Jew, who is also a Pole but who looks exactly like all the others, his expression is the same as all the rest of them.

The Dutch ship *Spaardam* – boarded in Rotterdam – is virtually a ghetto. Some of the companions are going to the United States, others will get off at Cuba, still others will travel on to Mexico. One will be lost in the countryside, another will go back to Russia, one will go on to Israel, another will end up in Australia.

'I made a friend during the voyage,' says my mother, 'she used to tell me all about her brother in Mexico, who used to say he was doing very well and had a lot of money. When we arrived I met him, he was a conductor on the Roma-Merida line. Yes, that wasn't much, but you don't know what the Roma-Merida line was like in those days, those early buses were smaller than bullock carts and the conductor had to go right round the bus every time it stopped saying "Roma-Merida, Roma-Merida": then he checked the tickets.'

'I felt good in Amsterdam,' says father, 'everything was so clean.'

'We had very little money and a lot of anxiety.'

'Why didn't you go on to the United States with the other passengers?'

'We couldn't. We thought we'd get off in Cuba and wait a while until the Americans gave us entry permits. By then, only my mother was allowed into the United States, even my sisters weren't. We always thought we'd go to Philadelphia and join the rest of the family.'

They reached Havana in mid-May. Even though it was dark, they decided to get off the boat and look round the city.

'It was so hot,' explains father,' the night was so dark and the negros were so black with their shining eyes and white, white teeth. I was really scared. It was so hot! Monstrously hot! We decided to go on to Mexico to see if the climate was normal there, and also because it was much closer to the United States.'

In Russia the summers were short and hot, the winters were long and white, as white as the negroes' teeth.

They were allowed to disembark at Veracruz with no visas and with nothing apart from some money lent them by the Dutch ship's purser. The ship was carrying three hundred and fifty immigrants. The chief officer lent them two hundred dollars to go through customs, dollars that had to be returned immediately so that he could lend them to other passengers who had no money either. My parents landed at Veracruz on 14 May 1925. Next day they went by train to Mexico City.

And that rather lengthy story explains how I come to be a citizen of Mexico.

24

The passports were long sheets of paper, official size, written on both sides, with a photo of a smiling young man exactly like my nephew Ariel, who turns out to be my father, the adolescent who married my mother and abruptly emigrated with her, like a flash of lightning (at least, that's how it must have seemed to my grandparents) to distant, tropical lands, never to be seen again. In order to leave Russia, my father had to part with some gold coins to people who could add or subtract a few years to his age when necessary. The age limit varied between twenty and twenty-four and he was twenty-two. Once two gold coins put him neatly in the nineteenth century. Another time gold provided him with the less dramatic, less significant date of 1904. The nineteenth century finally won out, and my father arrived in Mexico with a passport giving 1899 as his year of birth. My parents left for Moscow, where they stayed two months, from January to March 1925. They stayed in the home of one of my mother's relatives, who let out lodgings for young party members. The house had been turned into a barracks, like a hospital or a boarding school, with rows of beds separated by nothing more than sheets hung up to serve as curtains. They stayed there illegally. While they were in Moscow, my father was offered a civil service post, which he was entitled to because of his proletarian origins, having come from an agricultural community and having worked in the fields himself. My father preferred to continue to America, where his relatives were expecting him and where later, in November 1925, his mother finally arrived. When they got to Riga by train, they heard that entry into the United States was no longer open, so they decided to go to Cuba, because it was both easier and cheaper. They travelled through Berlin, and in Amsterdam they were met by an agent from Haias, the international Jewish association, who found them a place to stay and some money. My mother sold her dresses in Moscow, and that was the money they used to get to America.

'Did you think you'd ever go back to Russia one day?'

'No. You were quite free to leave Russia in those days. Your uncle was still able to leave in 1928, your uncle Volodia. It was just the start of the Stalin regime.'

'And I still remember Trotsky when he came through Odessa, on his way to the Crimea, all wrapped up in a huge cape,' says my father.

'In Amsterdam . . . no, it wasn't Amsterdam, it was Rotterdam, I came down with a fever and the Haias man brought me some cod liver oil tablets which were so big I couldn't swallow them. I kept them for years after we came to Mexico as a souvenir. At the end of our stay in that place the cheque I told you about came, and the others were all delighted about it and came to tell us the money had come, because some had come for them too. The ship was delayed in Santander, the last port of call before Havana, and that's where we changed our ticket because it cost an extra ten dollars for the fare and another four dollars for a Mexican visa. We couldn't land here without proving that we had one hundred dollars each. That was when the ship's officer, the second-in-command, gave me a packet with two hundred dollars in it for me and your father to clear customs. In fact, we only possessed fifteen dollars. It was so hot, and I really did feel very, very alone. We didn't know a soul and it was frightening. I had a smart black georgette dress that I'd bought with some of the money the relatives had sent to Rotterdam for us. It was so cold, you know what it's like in Mexico, it was 15 May. The first person we met in Cordoba was Kurtchansky, you know, Kurtchansky's father . . .'

'Mmmm, yes.'

'He was a pedlar, you know, someone who goes around selling things, like ties and buttons and such, he looked like nothing on earth, and the first thing he said to us was:

"Don't say you're Jews, say you're Germans." '

'Why was that?'

'Later on we said we were Russians, not Germans, I don't know why, but I felt bad saying I spoke German when I didn't. We arrived in Mexico and met the B'nai B'rith agent. They used to run a dormitory for single people, but since we were married we had to go to a hotel and . . . since we only had fifteen dollars, and we rented a room that cost thirty-five pesos a month, which was more than we had.'

'What did you live on?'

'Well, we managed to eat . . . we could use the kitchen. I used to go out and buy rolls, you got two for five pesos, and a bit of minced meat and I used to make *kokleten* and that's how we lived. I don't know if the B'nai B'rith people gave us anything or not.'

'I think they must have done, how else could you have managed?'

'Then we got a cheque from the family for five dollars. You know, they thought we were in the United States and that we could get work straight away in a factory. When I

opened the letter and saw there was only five dollars I felt
absolutely lost.'

25

'I travelled third class, that is, your father and I did. I
couldn't eat anything, because the food was so awful, even
though there were times when we went hungry. There was a
very bright woman who got on well with the purser and she
used to give us herring with vinegar and onions, and that
was a real treat. I sold everything in Moscow because I was
going to Cuba and Russian clothes wouldn't be any use over
there. I had some very smart grey suede shoes which were
open down the front and a pair of stockings that I had to
darn every day. In Holland we got some money from uncle
Ellis and I bought two dresses, a black crêpe one which was
very smart and one in lovely soft green wool.'

It's raining, San Miguel Regla is really beautiful, with its
gentle countryside and all the trees, the house with its
slender columns, that huge, friendly hacienda which I
almost like better than Marienbad, a place I've only ever
seen on film, except that I'm a bit of a snob and it seems
rather more exotic to me, as the mother of my Colombian
friend said, when we were in Paris and she was talking about
American clothes:

'They're so nice, they look so foreign.'

Mother goes on talking.

'Your father wasn't worried, in the daytime we stayed
under cover and at night we slept in our cabin. (And to
think that so much love can actually wear itself out!)

'There was a very interesting man travelling with us, a
very strange man, he spoke Russian but I think he was
born in Poland. We called him Miloshka, which means
"favourite". He disappeared when we got here,' she sighs,
then continues: 'You know, when we came to Mexico I

didn't know how to use earthenware pots, so at first I boiled milk in a pan a lot, and now I can't stand blenders, I prefer to mash things in an old Mexican earthenware bowl. You can get used to anything, that's for sure. Though I still don't know where I really am.'

'What do you mean?'

'I still can't take it in that I'm on my own now. I don't want to send your father's books away because it'll make the place seem so empty.'

'You should send his books, and his papers so they can be put in order and catalogued. I think it's the right thing to do, they'll be very useful for people who are trying to write the history of the Mexican Jewish community.'

The ground is wet. We have been sitting in a little garden, surrounded by cloistered arches, on antique style leather chairs, like the rest of the hacienda, like the bedrooms. Later we sit around the fireplace. The cleaning woman says softly, 'there's a bit of watery sunshine'. Everything is so peaceful, so lovely, so melancholy, I've eaten so much I can hardly move. I go out for a long walk, through the trees, past the pools, the remains of the old metal smelting furnace, and memories flood back with every step, memories of the former owner, the Marquis of Guadaloupe, Count of Regla, my mother's memories.

'That's how I learned to make strudl.'

'When did you learn that? Did you learn it at home? Did your mother teach you?'

'Yes, I learned quite a lot from her in Russia. In Tacuba Street, number 15, there was a restaurant and there was a Russian man who had emigrated there recently and he was chief cook, and I don't know how it came about, but I think I said to him that you could make strudl in the little coal-burning ovens, the portable ones, with two chimney vents and two openings, and they were making strudls and I made one and he liked it a lot . . .'

We go in because it is starting to rain.

'He said to me: "Such a lovely young woman with all sorts

of talents and she's interested in strudl." And I just got on and made it, and I don't even remember how much he paid me. We used to go to the club in the evenings. . .'

'You and the strudl man?'

'No, me and your father. We used to see Mr Perkis there, and Dr King and Katzenelson. Everybody changed their names. First they were living in the United States and then when the First World War broke out they went to Mexico to start again, and they founded the Young Men's Hebrew Association.'

'With an English name?'

'Yes, English because they'd just come from the United States, you see. They looked after us, in a way. Dr King used to give your father dental products, I've told you that already. And your father used to teach Hebrew at first to some of the children, our friends' children when they were preparing for their barmitzvahs. Some people were very kind, and we were very grateful to people too. Horacio Hinich's father, for example, taught natural sciences in the Yiddish school, but since I didn't know any Yiddish I couldn't even teach things I knew about.'

'So what did you know about?'

'Lots of things, I was always learning, I never seemed to stop. Playing the piano, science, art, even singing. But I ended up having to make strudl. That's the way it is. We brought lots of books instead of clothing, we had a basket of books that weighed sixty kilos. They were very important books and important people used to ask to borrow them and most of them we never set eyes on again. That's the way it is.'

'Do you still have any of those books?'

'Oh yes, there are a few left but I'm going to send them to Israel. There was a group of non-Jewish Russians here too, some very nice people, they were quite old, well, at least they seemed quite old to me.'

'How old were they?'

'I don't know, but they were a lot older than we were.

65

They lived in Xochimilco, which was a big place in those days, very beautiful with a lot of flowers everywhere and boats covered with greenery. They had a herb garden, they were typical Russians, very refined, honest, special people. There were some others who were former nobility.'

'What were their names? How could I forget? Oh, yes, they were called Sokolov.'

'Who were? The ones with the herb garden or the others?'

'No, the other ones, the nobility, were much younger. I don't remember what the others were called, but they had a little house in Xochimilco, it wasn't much more than a hut. They made us a typical Russian meal, they were so pleased to be able to speak Russian with someone.'

'Anything else, mother?'

'Oh, Margo, it all happened fifty years ago. Every night we used to go to the club, it didn't matter if you were on the right or on the left, nobody bothered. Then Abrams came, and he was an anarchist, a real leftist. It didn't matter what we did during the daytime to earn a living, because in the evenings we all went to the club.'

'Why didn't it matter what you did in the daytime?'

'Well, we sold bread, others were pedlars, street traders during the daytime, but in the evening we all came together for something better. There were all sorts of people, some as young as fourteen or fifteen. We all had to use Yiddish because we couldn't manage any other way. Some of them had come from Poland and some from Russia and some came from tiny little villages where they spoke a sort of Yiddish, and some even came from the United States and goodness knows what sort of English they could speak. So we all had to learn Yiddish, and when I started I couldn't understand anything because there were so many dialects, from Warsaw and Lithuania and Romania and Estonia and little Polish villages. I couldn't understand a word and then I started to learn gradually. Your father used to read to me, he was in bed a lot because he had trouble with his lungs and sometimes he used to cough up blood, and had to lie down because that frightened him. Your father used to read me Yiddish books, he used to translate them into Russian and that's how I learned. I knew the alphabet which I'd been taught when a little girl.'

'Didn't your mother speak Yiddish?'

'Of course she did, but she spoke a Ukrainian dialect, which was completely different. Later on all sorts of very well-educated young people used to come to our house.'

'Later on when?'

'Before I went to high school. They used to come to Odessa from their little villages to study and take important exams. I remember before the First World War one of those students was living in our house, a Zionist, who knew Hebrew perfectly, we put him up and fed him and he used to give us Hebrew lessons. He gave lessons to uncle Volodia, but I don't remember if Ilusha and I joined in. That's how I learned the alphabet. He went to Israel later. Your uncle Volodia told me he went on to become Minister of Finance.'

'In Israel?'

'Yes, in Israel. Uncle Volodia could remember his name, but I can't. I learned the alphabet and when I learned some words I wrote a letter to my parents. My mother wrote back in a terrible state because I'd suddenly written to her in Yiddish and she didn't think it could be me, she thought I must be dead, so then I wrote back again to her in Russian and calmed things down. That's what it's like when your children leave home . . .'

I come back to where I had been before. I go through the park, past the pools, and everything is damp, mildewed. It is slippery underfoot. There are flowers everywhere. I go over to a prickly pear tree and try to pluck some fruit. The pear defends itself and sticks its spikes in me. I go back to my room to try and pull out the prickles from my arms, my cheeks, the side of my mouth, my hands and my fingers. My father died, early in the morning of 3 January 1982.

26

'Do you feel very guilty about leaving Russia?'

'Not guilty, no. Obviously I felt sad about my family, but when I came to Mexico I felt so free, I used to walk down the Zocalo, it was May when we got here and in September there were the national fiestas and I found it all very moving. I didn't miss Russia itself, because we'd left quite legally. The problems only started when Stalin came to power.'

'Didn't you miss your family?'

'Well of course I did, what a silly thing to ask! When I was studying chemistry, for example, they used to like me a lot, I was the secretary of all my group. Most of the young people were Jewish, but there were some who belonged to the Komsomol, the young communists and gradually they started trying to make me join, but somehow it didn't appeal to me much, there weren't many girls involved and they all seemed so gloomy, I think they even wore boots and trousers. Not smart boots mind, they were too dismal for that. They had rifles that were not just for show, and I felt they were against me: either you joined the party or you were nobody. They thought of me as a member of the middle classes, somebody with no place in society. Had I joined the party things would have been very different, but I felt I was being pressured, I wasn't free to take my own decisions.'

'Is that why you preferred life in Mexico?'

'No, I didn't know then I would be going to Mexico, I just wanted to leave, that's all there was to it. When I got to Mexico I felt a lot freer. We both did. Your father was a political bureaucrat, but I know that when he came to our house he used to feel at ease too, because he never really adapted to party life and in Russia in those days if you were outside the party you were outside everything. In Mexico, whether you were or were not a party member was not such a big deal.'

'How was it that though you were the only girl in the family with all those brothers, you were the one who wanted to leave?'

'Because I only had brothers, that's why.'

'Yes, but why didn't they want to leave too?'

'I was the first one to go from our family. We didn't have anyone abroad, whereas a lot of people had whole families overseas. I don't really know if any of them wanted to go or not. I suppose that if you were free to go where you liked, many people never wanted to go anywhere because they had no idea where to go. It was a tragedy for my family, because I was the only daughter and also because I was going somewhere completely unknown. We had a cousin in the United States, but we never heard from him.'

'What about the one in Argentina?'

'There were the Midhzibosky, true, but your father didn't want to go down there, he wanted to join his family in the United States. We never thought about going to Mexico. Afterwards when your aunts arrived we were a tribe of more than fifty people, though sadly we've lost some of them now, including your father . . .'

27

We talk on the telephone every day without fail. It's practically a holy rite, even though sometimes it's like listening to rain drip off a duck's back. Father says:

'What are you up to? Why aren't you coming over? How are the girls? Are you coming on Sunday? really? oh, that's great.'

Mother picks up the extension and her voice sounds so youthful, like it did when I was a child. My mother used to wear starched white linen collars, or beautifully worked crocheted ones, and she wore a rose fastened near her neckline or on one side, and some fox furs that I still have

Mother and Lilly, my older sister, 1929

for Renata to play with. Mother started to wear make-up when I was ten years old, but only red lipstick, and she used to go out looking lovely with her rose and her foxes. She had long thick hair pulled back off her face, but she never wore glasses even though she was very short-sighted; later when she did start wearing them she cut her hair too. It completely changed her image. I remember her affectionately, as I do my father, who had no beard in those days, and who wore round horn-rimmed glasses that I keep now on my bedroom wall with the photos and the pictures of him, with his blue eyes that were always so mischievous, chatting to Dr Reinking, the nose and throat specialist, both men talking about a woman and laughing: 'She had such a big zhopa'. Now I know that 'zhopa' means backside and 'curve' means whore, a word my mother used in a low voice when my parents were arguing and I used to gaze at them without really understanding what they were fighting about. Fixed in my mind as a huge, recurring image is the necklace I never saw round my mother's neck, because it was so enormous, a huge length of necklace comprising dozens of oval shaped red beads that smelled of amber and which my aunts had brought back from Constantinople with them as a present. We used to play with it in the old art deco bedroom all in heavy ochre coloured wood, with dark, almost black grains, attracted by the cosy feather mattresses that my grandmother Ethel had given to my mother as a dowry. You could lose sight of all sorts of things in there.

My mother once gave me the necklace, shortened somewhat, after I'd been away for a long time. After my younger sister Shulamis had been away on another occasion she asked me to lend it and then gave it to her, a fact that I still find hard to swallow. It's difficult to erase certain faces and certain things from your memory, especially when they leave a nasty mark in the family album.

The telephone rings. It's my father's voice, and he almost never calls me, it's my mother who makes the daily phone call. He asks:

'What are you reading?'

'I'm reading Pilnyak.'

'Boris Pilnyak, he was in Odessa in 1924. At a meeting. Which book of his are you reading?'

'*Mahogany*.'

'I don't know that one. I'm still reading away every day, right now I'm reading a poet who sent me his works about fifteen years ago. Weinberg is his name, I saw him in Israel, but I didn't read him then because I didn't much like him. It's a shame, because I'm really enjoying him now. He writes well, he's a good poet. I'd like you to read me the story of what you're doing. When are coming over? ... on Sunday? ... great, but you really mean it, don't you? You'd better! *Zai gesunt*.'

When we meet he asks me again:

'What are you reading?' I answer: '*Mahogany*, it's translated by Sergio Pitol.'

'You're wrong there, Pitol knows Polish, he was in the embassy there. I know him well, he's a fine writer. But he doesn't know any Russian.'

'Yes, Dad, he knows Russian well; he was in Russia too for several years and that's how he learned the language. He's translating Chekhov next.'

'Really? That's great, you should bring him over so we can have a chat and I'll see what his accent's like. Boris Pilnyak was very well-known. He came from the north originally, his background was German.'

'Did you talk to him?'

'I did. He told me about his latest book. I can't remember what it was called but it was all about sex. How can I remember details like that after such a long time? I don't know what happened to him later, but at that time his books weren't banned.'

'He was sent to Siberia and he died out there.'

'Who told you that?'

'Sergio Pitol.'

'He was a nice looking man, very intelligent, who knew a

lot. He introduced a new style of writing.'

'Was he tall?' (That's one of my hang-ups.)

'No, middling. There was a meeting. I used to go and listen to all the writers. It was in Zeifulina's time. Who was she? She was a great poet. She came from the north too, she belonged to another generation. At that time there were new writers introducing new styles, writing quite differently, just like the revolution, they were revolutionary writers. That was in Babel's day. I'll see if I have any of his books, I think I do, from 1924, just think of that! He was very new in those days, he was about thirty.'

'Yes, he was born in 1894.'

'You see? What did I tell you? I met Andrei Biely, his name means "white", then too, and there was another one, Sasha Tchorniy, pronounced with a long Y. His name means black, so there was a white one and a black one. Biely was one of the first who learned to write verse in the new revolutionary style. We met him in 1923, he came from the north too. Zeifulina came from Siberia, from the real north. Zeifulina . . . I don't remember what her first name was, I think it was Sofia . . . no, it wasn't Sofia . . . it'll come to me. Andrei Biely was a symbolist, he wasn't a very easy writer, in fact you could hardly understand anything he wrote, but it was interesting. Tchorniy, the one with the long Y, he toned everything down eventually. I think I may have some of his books, he used to write satire. I've got some of Pilnyak's books too, but not *Mahogany*. Bagritzky was there too, he was a Jew.'

'Yes, you told me that.'

'But I didn't tell you what he said when I was coming to Mexico, did I? He said: "There are no returns from there." He belonged to the southern writers' society and they used to invite other writers to come along and talk about their work. Those meetings were always full, people were very enthusiastic about them. Osip Osipovich was the boss, he was a poet of the old generation, much more famous than Biely, though Biely was better known that Pilnyak, he was

MARGO GLANTZ

one of Alexander Blok's generation, you know, the symbolist
poet. And, Akhmahtova's husband, Gumilyov, too, spelt
with a Y which makes a word sound soft, like the double ll
in Spanish. Oh, they were fantastic years! There still wasn't
a hard line in those days, everybody was trying out
something new. Does Sergio know Russian?'

'Yes, Dad, he knows it very well.'

'Are you sure about that? He knows Polish. Is he a
communist?'

'He's on the left.'

'He's in Poland though . . . no, he's here, I saw you with
him, in the Porrua bookshop down San Angel, when we
were together last June, yes, he came over and said hello,
he's a friendly sort of man. He's a good writer, he'll do a good
job with Pilnyak. I met Sergio in the forties.'

'No, you didn't, Dad. Sergio was only born in 1933.'

'Oh, yes, you're right.' There's a mysterious noise, then he
starts talking in a confused way: 'He's a Mexican, isn't he?'

'Yes, and his parents were Italian.'

'Yes, Sergio Pitol's a good writer. I'd like to see him, bring
him over.'

28

The first Mexicans that my father met, apart from his
customers, his neighbours and his employers, were writers.

'Did you know Gonzalez Martinez?'

He knew him well, and even wrote an unpublished
preface for his collection of poems, Cantares. 'I used to keep
it in one of the chests, but I can't find it. When I knew him
he was living in the suburb of Santa Maria, and then he
moved out to the Valle.

'I knew Gonzalez Martinez' son too, Gonzalez Rojo,
another very fine poet who died young, and I even knew his
grandson. And I saw a lot of Mariano Azuela. He was a

doctor when I met him.'

'How did you meet?'

'I met him because he gave me his novel *The Underdogs*.'

'That's not really an answer. Who introduced you?'

'I don't remember. All I know is I met him. I went to his house in Santa Maria. They used to look at me very oddly there, a Jewish poet was a rare sight. He signed the copy he gave me. Senora Tfass has that book right now. She borrowed it and you'll have to ask her to give it back.'

'What was his house like?'

'How did he live? How do you say, as a "klein burger", middle class. He lived a normal life like any other family, he had a lot of books and a piano. In those days he was one of Mexico's leading revolutionary writers. I knew lots of writers, I used to want to know all of them back then. I don't know where I met them all.'

'In cafés,' mother interrupts.

'No, I didn't meet Azuela in a cafe, he never went to cafés. He didn't like intellectuals.'

'Maybe it was through the Contemporaneo group?'

'I met Jaime Torres Bodet and Villarrutia at the Café Paris and sometimes I used to talk to them, and I saw Agustin Lazo from a distance, he was a very big man. Octavio Paz was younger and didn't mix with them much, he used to stay on the sidelines. Lazo lived at number 30, Isabel La Catolica Street, right where señor Hinich had his clothing store.'

'Did you know Cuesta? He was one of the Contemporaneos too, wasn't he? He married Lupe Marin, after she left Rivera.'

'Yes, I did. Jorge Cuesta. I met him at the Café Paris. I used to go there every day. And I met Rafael Lopez . . .'

'You've told me that . . .'

'It doesn't matter . . . I met Rafael Lopez who was working in the National Museum in Moneda Street. They were the big names in those days. People were still talking about Lopez Velarde who I never met, he'd died by then. They were always talking about him in the Café Paris.'

'What did they used to say?'

'They used to say he was a genius, they'd all been fond of him and felt bad that he'd died so young.'

'Have you read anything by him?'

'Of course I have! He's so romantic ... all that about trains looking like toys . . . everybody used to quote Lopez Velarde.'

'Did you meet any other younger poets? Like Efrain Huerta?'

'Yes, a lot, but Gonzalez Martinez was the most ...'

'Dad, you've already told me about him. Have you read everything he's written?'

'Of course. I read his poetry because I found it interesting and the others were interested in talking about the Russian poets I knew. Like Alexander Blok, though I have to go back a long way ... Well, I knew them all, Eduard Bagritsky, and Furmanov. There were two, one called Dimitri and I can't remember the other one's name ... the first one was in the army, I didn't meet him, I met the other one ... what was his name? ... I've forgotten it. I remember another poet, called Brodsky. He was very good, but we'd better leave him be. I'll get some material out for you, I ought to remember, I can't just ramble on like this ...'

29

Selling clothing is one of the oldest Jewish trades, and a great many Jews have been involved in it, like those who used to sell in the markets at Vilna or Minsk, or Łodz or Kiev. Even my father tried it once. Equipped with ties, handkerchiefs, socks and underpants he tried to become a door-to-door salesman, but had to give it up because the ladies didn't understand what he was after.

'They used to imagine all sorts of things. I remember my friend Isaac Babel in Russia, the one who was banned later, but in those days our writers' group used to read a chapter from some book or other. Once I was reading when the Makhno anarchists killed a young Jewish lad, a red guard, and he was left lying there in the street, stark naked, and the girls went out to have a look at the blond curly hair round his you know what.'

'So what about the ladies? Did you sell them underpants?'

'No, I sold all kinds of clothing. Dr King recommended me to Jaime Hinich, Dr Horacio Hinich's father, and he sold women's knickers and gave me a pair to sell for him. But it didn't work out because they had laces and the ladies said laces would get caught.'

'Didn't they want them with laces?'

'Not unless I showed them how to thread their laces through the holes, but I didn't know any Spanish (I still don't know that much). There were some tough women in Chihuahua Street, some really tough women, they certainly didn't part easily with anything they had, least of all their money. They were quite something, they were.'

Repeating something dozens of times sharpens the memory, but memories are deceitful even if you do go back over them dozens of times in your own mind. Jacob denies some of the details he had recalled previously, and the knickers with laces are transformed simply into delicate Swiss lace that doesn't need tying and doesn't decorate anything. My father says that he can recall events from his childhood with more detail every time he tries, but that almost everything that happened later is forgotten. Sometimes he revives a bit of it and I seize upon it like a vulture.

When my sister Lilly was born, señora Hinich gave my mother twelve dozen tiny Swiss socks, absolutely minute and beautifully made, all size 1. My sister was never able to use them, because following the advice of a Russian doctor, who must have been rather like the troublesome Dr Spock who ruined three generations of children in the United States and some middle class Mexicans into the bargain, my mother kept us muffled up in straitjackets with bound feet.

'I remember, I was struggling to bring all of you up following Dr Dhzuck's book. Dr Ovadiev lived in Mexico and years later I met him when Susana was born. The book said that you should swaddle babies in strips of cloth.'

I presume we must have experienced being a fetus twice over and my ancestors must be immortal, since they knew what it felt like to be in the grave.

And that was the end of my family's experiment with the clothing trade.

30

'We didn't know any Spanish at all and señor King gave me dental products to sell, because he owned a company that made them. What a coincidence that was! I worked as a dentist later, because in those days people weren't used to the idea of cleaning their teeth. We were very worried, we didn't know what to do.'

'And then señor Perkis came, he was very bright and he saw what was going on right away and sent us to a European breadshop, the one that belonged to Burakoff (he still spells his name like that), the first breadmaker to produce Central European type bread.'

'We had a wicker box and I started selling bread. Now where's that photo?'

'I don't know, I'll have to look for it. Your father was selling bread and he didn't know any Spanish, but they bought it, presumably out of pity.'

'I made quite a lot of money. I made nine centavos on every loaf. You could get two rolls for five centavos then. I didn't sell rolls, I sold plaited long loaves and rye bread.'

'You used to sell plaited loaves, did you?'

'Yes, people really enjoyed them. Your uncle's bakery was in Loreto Street, number 8.

'One day there was a huge downpour, it was the rainy

season you see, and your father came home soaked through, he had to take off his trousers to dry them because they were his only pair. The bread was completely ruined.'

'I was very young, I was only about twenty-three. They all used to make fun of my wicker box, so I traded it in for one of those Mexican baskets, the round ones you carry on your head.'

'Yes,' says my mother, laughing, 'because the poor boy was carrying the box with a rope round his forehead, and he could just put the basket on his head. That's how we got bread and food and other little things.'

'Señor Perkis's job was a stroke of good luck, because otherwise I couldn't have earned a living wage. He came to see us often and used to bring us things, he'd stay a little while, he liked coming to our place.'

'We were living at 38 Soledad Street,' says mother again, 'we had twenty rooms, twenty homes.'

Things changed gradually and my father managed to build up his list of customers. Carts pulled by mules or donkeys used to go along Loreto Street, and the Russian conductor used to be on one of them, my mother's friend's brother, the one who was doing well in Mexico and who later went back to the Soviet Union where he disappeared. Mexico City reached as far as 178 Coahuila Street in 1926, where there was one solitary house belonging to a doctor who lived with his old mother, and she used to buy the bread my father sold, the long plaited loaves. He used to ride into the city on horseback, and when sales improved he took on an assistant, Serafin, an Oaxaca Indian.

'I didn't have Serafin at first, there was another one. I used to pay him 1.50 pesos a day which was a lot of money in those days. I used to sell bread on credit. I'd leave the bread and they'd pay me later. Once I went to collect some money that was owing to me on the corner of Alvaro Obregon Street and Jalapa. It was an old house with a garden. A tinsmith lived there and I just went in, I didn't know that you weren't supposed to just go into other people's houses over here, and the man was big and tough and he started hitting me. He hit me three times and left me covered in blood and crying like a baby. Like an idiot I went off to the police and brought back two policemen; but I couldn't understand a word of what he said to them. He never paid me a cent, he just thumped me.'

And so my father complied with Biblical advice and earned his daily bread with the sweat of his brow.

'Sometimes I'd sit and read poetry on a bench. Serafin was a great help to me, he knew all my customers. I used to read in Spanish. I could only understand one word in ten, because the rhythm of Spanish was so completely different to Russian poetry. Once a Uruguayan poet came to see me, and I also read Diaz Miron's *Lascas*. He was pretty tough and aggressive. Later on I personally met the poet Solon de Mel, which was the pseudonym used by Gonzalo Luzuriaga, one of the leading men in the government. He was a lousy poet.'

My father doesn't understand politics at all.

'I came here when I was twenty-two and now I'm eighty.'

'That's a whole lifetime.'

'It's more than a lifetime, we're very very old at eighty. We were just a couple of kids when we came out here.'

31

In September 1925 on the eve of Yom Kippur, my parents are drinking tea instead of taking part in the *kol nidre* service, the hymn to the dead, when sins are confessed in the synagogue. Next day they go to Xochimilco for the first time. At this point my own recollections start to intrude: I remember those everlasting, ceremonial Sundays when all the family packed in to one of the little streetcars or my father stopped a rickety old taxi, asking what the trip would cost and after a lengthy argument the driver would agree to fifty cents. Afterwards would come the

My mother and father when they arrived in Mexico:
carnival time

flower-decked boats, the mariachi bands, beer, and clearest of all, the hard boiled eggs and the *kokleten* (chicken meat balls).

My parents hired an old car, which had four doors and no glass in the windows, with plastic covers that you could fit in if it rained. There weren't many people about, it was a weekday, there were a few boats, a lot of flowers, the ritual photos.

On the way home, with everybody very cheerful, the driver hit a tree and turned the car over. It came to a halt in a ditch full of filthy, stagnant water, crawling with bugs. Mother was trapped in her seat, and only her head was visible sticking out of the water. They were with a couple about ten years older — 'they seemed very old to me' — whose name was Langzam and who later went out to Australia. The driver disappeared and since they were out at Cuautitlan some peasants came and lifted out the car.

'When they pulled me out, I said in Russian: "It's nothing, really," and they all looked at me as if I were a hero. I was still wearing my old moss-green Russian school uniform. They wrapped me in a raincoat and we went home. We were living with a Russian Jewish couple, he was a dentist (just for a change) and what's more, they were very religious.'

It's a sin to go on a journey on the Sabbath or on any religious day. They expiated the sin later by collecting money for Jews displaced during the war: in 1947 or 1948. Once they got on a plane to fly across lake Titicaca, over Guayaquil and land in Atalaya, the oil producing area in Peru, where the oil is loaded and the heat is unbearable. The plane took off, left the ground and then crashed down into the mud.

'They got us out through the pilot's emergency exit. One of the other passengers was an Indian woman with very long hair tied back in a pony tail crying her eyes out and fidgeting with her rosary beads. I asked her why she was crying and she said it was because she was afraid of flying.

"So why do you fly then?" '

'Because it's so exciting.'

Another trip was in the first Braniff intercontinental two-tier airliner, with the passengers on top and the bar down in the plane's belly, flying over Brazil from Belem to Pernambuco, over the forest, the Mato Grosso, 'the treetops were all joined together, rising out of the mud and you could see little canoes and strange people in them, and then they told us that we were looking for a missing plane, and we searched for three hours and couldn't find anything. All we saw were strange animals and people living down there in the virgin forest.'

Great cities and cities lost from the map. In the state of São Paulo there is a tiny village where all the inhabitants are lepers.

'There was a Jew living there married to a leper woman. He took me back to his house for a meal, but I didn't know what was happening and the other Jews round there never told me anything. I made a few jokes and said they could ring some extra bells for me because I was unclean too. A tall woman came in, wearing long white gloves with some marks on her face, and her husband had come from Bessarabia, on the banks of the Dniester. He owned almost all the village and she was pretty wealthy too, he was the head man in that village. He gave me a lot of money to go and have a meal with him. Afterwards, when I learned that they were lepers I was scared they might have infected me too. I went to a dermatologist in Rio, Dr Bronstein, and he assured me that you can only catch leprosy through sexual contact or if you have open wounds in your skin, and the incubation period is seven years. I didn't stop worrying till my seven years were up.'

32

Soon after my parents arrived in Mexico my father started having sharp pains in his stomach and an English doctor decided that it was Montezuma's revenge. Another doctor had a better idea and diagnosed an ulcer, but another even more determined doctor, a German Jewish doctor called Ulfelder, took him into hospital and took out his appendix.

'When he was ill, since we didn't have a telephone I had to go half way across town to see the doctor. And the doctor asked me how had I dared to go all that way on foot with my heart problem. All I had was a cold. I've never had heart trouble in my life.'

In spite of the different diagnoses and in spite of the different nationalities of all the doctors, my father was operated on for appendicitis, though his illness was nothing more than an ordinary infection of amoeba. He was taken into the English Hospital which cost six pesos a day, in ward 28 which had eight beds.

Señor Filler loaned my mother fifty pesos, exactly the cost of the stay in hospital. While my father was ill, my mother used to go out and sell bread with Serafin, the short, well-built young man from Oaxaca who used to laugh all the time whenever he heard my father mangling Spanish. Everybody looked at my mother as if she were a Martian, selling bread from door to door in her smart clothes.

'Everybody was very surprised to see me in the truck, one of those little squat truck-buses with a conductor who shouted: "Roma-Merida, Roma-Merida". We put the basket on the roof and since I was there very early, the conductor used to call me the early bird. I didn't understand what he said, but it made an impression on me and I thought it was rude. Then I went round with the delivery man and in the afternoon I went to the English Hospital which was out in the sticks, in the place that's now called Polanco.'

33

You know, I think that in our heart of hearts we all have some links with Franz Kafka. Or at least with *The Trial*. That's why my father often tells me, getting very excited every time, about his brushes with the law. After all the changes in Russia that led him to this lovely ancient place that is Mexico City, my father became involved over here with leftist groups, and eventually with the anarchists.

It is a good thing to remember, and the theatres in this city remember a great deal. They still show or rather perform the story of Sacco and Vanzetti, which when I was little sounded to me like a single name. A name that was later to be linked with that of the Rosenbergs, who died in the electric chair supposedly for treason. That was when I was a teenager and used to take part in demonstrations for all sorts of lost causes.

My father went to a literary-political evening event in honour of the murdered Italians, which was held at 31 Palma Street towards the end of 1927. At that meeting there was a speech by Abrams, an anarchist who had gone back to

Russia after being expelled from the United States (and for some reason that nobody can remember was passing through Mexico) because he had supported in writing Nicola Sacco and Bartolomeo Vanzetti who were executed on 23 August 1927 in a Massachusetts jail, accused of theft and murder and not of having unacceptable political views. Abrams talked about a book called *America Against Abrams*, which gave an account of his trial and deportation because he had taken a stand against the American legal system on behalf of the men who were executed. My father read a poem that was later published in a New York Jewish anarchist journal, *Frier Arbeiter Stime (The Free Worker's Voice)*. A detective was present at the meeting who was employed by the chief of police and when it was over he arrested my father along with Abrams. Jacob was held in custody seventy-two hours, and at first he was with four prisoners arrested for ordinary offences. When he protested they put him on his own in a corridor, if you can call being alone being surrounded by gigantic bugs that infested the bed and strolled up and down the walls. Even worse, abnormally big rats strolled across the bed too, and across the prisoner.

'All I could do was keep quite still.'

Sam Wisniak, who died not long ago, found out about the arrest and came to intervene on my father's behalf. Wisniak, 'a really decent man,' used to work for the army, he made caps for them and because of that he had a lot of influence.

When Wisniak came to get my father out, one of the guards, whose name was Cruz, said:

'You Jews always help each other out.'

Meanwhile my mother had been rushing all over the place.

Jacob tried to intervene for Abrams, but Wisniak said:

'I'm not getting him out because I don't know him, I heard they'd arrested you, Yasha, so I came to get you, because I know damn well you're no anarchist, even though you write those crazy poems sometimes.'

'Abrams was a *shlimazl*,' says my mother.

'A *shlimazl*? No, he was unlucky, he was an idealist.'

My father finishes his story, repeating:

'Wisniak was a great man.'

Abrams stayed with the rats for a while longer.

34

'I used to get on very well with painters. I knew Siqueiros well, and Fernando Leal who hardly ever spoke, but that was after.'

'After what?'

'After I used to go to the Café Paris. Leal painted a picture, well, you should call it a mural really, in Salubridad, and then they painted over it because it was pornographic, there were rabbits in it. He knew all of you girls, he used to come to our house a lot. And I was friends with another painter, Bulmaro Guzman. Diego Rivera was talking to me just two or three days before he died, he came to see us with his brushes in hand. He'd rung the restaurant first to make sure I'd be there. When I saw him, his right hand was paralyzed. "I want to paint you, Jacob," he said, and I said: "Wait until your hand's better." It's a shame, because he could have painted me with his left hand too.'

They first met Rivera with Alexandra Kollontai, they had gone to Academia Street, to the Russian club.

'She was a very interesting woman, she used to ride well,' intervenes mother, 'such an interesting woman, not an official Party type at all, because in those days the women in the Communist Party used to wear boots and carry guns. She was very, very womanly, an Amazon who wore gloves, an aristocrat, she wasn't working class by any means. She wasn't a peasant, she was special . . . I don't know why they sent her here as ambassador.'

'Kollontai was a full member of government, and

Lunacharsky was Minister of Culture at that time and she was his mistress,' explains father.

'She was always so beautifully dressed, it was amazing. That's the one thing I remember,' says mother, still going on. 'I have to admit that.'

'And then Eisenstein and Mayakovsky came to Mexico,' father intervenes.

'Which one of them did you think was the more interesting?'

'They were both completely different. I stayed up all night with Mayakovsky, until two or three in the morning. We went out to the hill, Estrella Hill, which was outside the town in those days, and we sat in the open and talked about poetry and recited poems to each other. We talked about Futurism and Imagism, which were fashionable then, and about Marinetti and another poet, a working class poet, Aseyev, and we recited his poem entitled "War" which he wrote in 1914.'

My father used to recite it often back then; now he adds bits, and has to keep stopping as he tries to recall it. He was surprised that Mayakovsky was amazed at the fact that a young man who didn't live in Russia should know Russian poetry so well. Yankl recalls his highly poetical youth: 'Only two youngsters could spend all night walking around talking about literature.'

'He was tall, well-built and handsome and he made a big impression on me. I even recited some of my poems to him. I was short and skinny.

'I didn't see much of Eisenstein. I congratulated him at a Dadaist reception in his honour at the Soviet Embassy...or was it in the Russian club...?

'He was an extraordinary man, very handsome, such an interesting man, a real character, and he didn't have any rigid opinions, he was so energetic, he was a man with a vision ahead of his time. He'd made a few fragments of *Storm over Mexico*, which later on was turned into *Viva Mexico*.'

My father as a thinker

35

When I was very small, my father had a beard. It made him look like a younger version of Trotsky. They killed Trotsky, and, after, when I went out with my father people used to say: 'Look, there goes Trotsky and his daughter.' It frightened me and I didn't like going out with him. Before he died, Diego Rivera said to my father: 'You look more like him every day.' My parents agree that Rivera's Russian was not perfect but his bad accent made it sound very exotic.

In January 1939, my father was attacked by a fascist group of Golden Shirts who had collected in 16 September Street where my parents had a little boutique called Lisette where they sold bags and gloves. His beard, his Jewish appearance and maybe even his resemblance to Trotsky made Jacob Glantz the perfect target for a local pogrom or lynching. Some of them tried to push him onto the tram lines, whilst others threw stones and shouted traditional insults. My father managed to escape with the help of some astonished passers-by and dashed into the boutique and up into the attic. Siqueiros's brother who happened to be passing and had gone to say hello to my parents (he used to sell engravings done by his brother) planted himself in the doorway with both arms out shouting: 'Try and hit me!' Meanwhile my mother, who claims she didn't look Jewish because of her black hair ('there were no white hairs in it in those days') managed to get out with a blonde shop assistant, who was also Jewish, and go to the tailor's next door to ring for help. The shop door was made of glass and the demonstrators were throwing stones and my father was hit on the forehead. After a while the firemen arrived with their chief (my mother thinks his name was General Montes) and helped my father get out of the shop. My father was moaning in terror and one of the firemen said: 'Don't cry, Jew, we've come to save you.' They wrapped him in a black cape, picked him up like a baby and carried him out to the fire-engine. My mother managed to lower the metal

My maternal grandparents

screen door with the help of some friends, including the brother of Siqueiros who I think was still in prison then for having threatened to kill Trotsky.

My father came to our apartment in Zaragoza Street which we had just moved into (my mother remembers that she had broken a mirror just a few days beforehand). I saw him in bed with his forehead all bloody and surrounded by a lot of people with frightened looks on their faces. When they found they couldn't lynch him, the fascists raced round to San Juan de Letran Street where one of my uncles sold fresh fruit drinks. They threw stones at him too, insulted him and broke his glass barrels of fresh water. Then the crazed mob of Golden Shirts poured into other streets in the centre and stoned any shops they found. My parents' house was transformed into a refuge and meeting point. The following day my parents' photographs were headline news in the papers. I remember one in particular in *La Prensa*, where Jacob stood out, his pointed chestnut-coloured beard making him look very Jewish.

A few days later my father left for the United States to visit his brothers in Philadelphia for the first time (if you look in a telephone book for that city, you'll find as many Glantzes as there are Lopezes here in Mexico, practically half the city are cousins of mine). We stayed behind with my grandmother, who was very ill by then, and my mother, who was very frightened. The impression of that fear and the image of my father with his beard and blood all over his forehead have stayed with me for years. My father came back a few months later. The Second World War was raging and he had shaved off his beard.

36

Living with someone probably means losing part of your own identity. Living with someone contaminates; my father alters my mother's childhood and she loses her patience listening to accounts of my father's childhood. Once we had all gone to the cemetery on the first anniversary of my uncle's death and Lucia recalled the attempted pogrom that my father had experienced. So I asked him to tell me what had happened to him:

'I was working in the Jewish Charity Association at 21 Gante Street, on the corner of Venustiano Carranza that used to be called Capuchinas, and your mother had her shop called Lisette on 16 September Street, number 29, selling ladies' bags and gloves. I came out of the charity place and there was a big meeting underway (it was January 1939). I was on my way to the shop when I met a young man called Salas, he knew who I was, he'd been a student in Germany and spoke very good German. He came towards me with two other lads and he yelled: "Death to the Jews. Jews out of

Mexico!" I had a willow stick with me, and I broke it over his head and it split into three. He grabbed it out of my hand and tried to push me in front of a tram, but I held onto a lamp-post and wouldn't let go. I don't know how I managed to break free and run to the shop, which was shut, though the steel door wasn't in place.

'The police came right away, I don't remember how many there were, there could have been fifty or a hundred, and Siqueiros's brother; if he hadn't been there I'd have been killed. He said to me: "They'll have to get me before they get you, Jacob," and he stretched both arms out wide. He was a giant of a man. They had a truck outside full of stones and they were throwing them at the shop and they smashed the shop window and took everything they could get. I don't know how I got out of there.'

'Where was mother?'

'She'd got out with the assistant. There were stones flying all over the place, I didn't know where to hide, because everywhere I went there were more stones. I thought I'd never get out of there, I thought I was done for, there was nothing I could do. There were so many people outside and so many stones and I was covered in blood. There was a man called Osorio outside, a Cuban that I knew quite well, and he stood up on a platform and made a Hitler-type speech, and even though he knew me he spoke against me and against Jews in general. When they ran out of stones, they went to San Juan de Letran where your uncle Mendel had his drinks stand and they came back with great chunks of ice which they started throwing at me, and a massive lump of ice hit me on the head and that was a sign from God, because the ice saved me. I was bleeding heavily, because I'd been hit on the head, and the ice stopped the bleeding. I wouldn't have survived without that ice.'

'Where were we?'

'You were all very little, I don't think you ever saw any of that. General Montes appeared later and he put his cloak round me and said: "Don't cry, Jew, I'm here to save you." '

Is the pleasure of remembering somehow debilitating? Maybe memory gets weakened by being handled and stretched so much. Memories return so often and we stay hooked onto some event or other, standing like my father did when he spent whole days watching Orozco or Rivera painting those never-ending frescoes in the National Palace or the Bellas Artes.

'Why were you so interested in art, especially in painting and sculpture?'

'Because I'd always been around artists ever since I was a little boy, first in Russia and then over here.'

'Did you know Orozco?'

'Yes, I knew him. He was a very rigid man, very, I don't know, he wasn't very friendly. Rivera was a lot better, we were actually friends. Yes, Rivera used to speak very good Russian. I saw him just a week before he died and he said ...'

'You've already told me that. You keep telling me the same things!'

'I used to spend whole days watching Orozco when he was painting the mural in the Bellas Artes and he didn't talk much, he wasn't a very talkative man at all. Rivera used to talk a lot though. He used me as his model for Trotsky. I wasn't exactly Trotsky, but I was there with him watching all the time and that inspired him to paint the young Trotsky. He didn't usually allow people to watch him while he was painting, but he let me in and I saw all his early sketches.'

'And did you ever hear Orozco say anything?'

'Yes, he used to talk sometimes, he painted with just one hand.'

'And did Diego paint with both hands?'

'He certainly did, Rivera used both hands and Orozco only used one, he was a tough man, a country type. Orozco had some strange models, there was a whore who used to walk the streets in Tacuba, next to the main Post Office, and he'd paint her with her legs spread open. He had some strange ideas.'

'What did you talk about with him?'

'He didn't talk much, but he said he found working class people very interesting.'

'Were you on good terms? Did he call you by your first name?'

'No, never, I was very respectful towards him. I was on first name terms with Rivera, and with Fernando Leal when he was painting the frescoes in the Preparatoria. They made him wipe off a mural because he'd painted doves making love and that was considered very improper. There was a big scandal and later on they restored the mural, but without the doves.'

'You told me about that too.'

'I've got a picture he did at home, it's a photo because the original got lost in one of the moves, or maybe it was just misplaced. He painted me as a Russian soldier.'

'Why were you painted so often?' (In my house there are about a hundred and thirty paintings of my father, without counting the hundreds of self-portraits he did himself.)

'Because they all wanted to paint me. I appealed to painters, I was very paintable.'

'And what did mother say when you used to go and watch painters at work?'

'What could she say? I always felt at home with artists. I knew Ignacio Rosas. I was working in the same place as him, on Motolinia (I think it was number 8) and 5th of May, where the Bank of Mexico is now, in an old house. I'd been working for the Jewish Charity people since the early thirties.'

'Weren't you a dentist by then?'

'On and off. We had a shoeshop too in Tacuba, and then we had the boutique. I was secretary of the Jewish Charity Association until 1939 when I was attacked by the Golden Shirts, and after that I went to the United States for three months and left my job. Rosas was a great portrait painter.

He did several portraits of me.'

My father smiles like Narcissus, sitting at a table surrounded by a dozen little Jacobs all looking at one another.

Next Saturday, as usual, I go over again. My father looks at one of his portraits with great satisfaction and great attention:

'How interesting,' he says. 'You can tell he's a poet.'

38

'Last night I dreamed I was writing a poem, or rather a dozen poems. They were really good, but when I woke up I couldn't remember any of them. When I came to Mexico, before I thought about earning a living I was already thinking about poetry. That's why I sought out people who could think. When I arrived neither Hebrew nor Russian were any use at all. I remembered Luis de Carvajal's *The Young Man*. He used to write in Spanish, because there was no Hebrew literary language over here.

'Then I started writing in Yiddish, but that language wasn't very much used either.' (Whereas it was in New York, where the great Jewish poets, such as Leivik, all lived, and great novelists like Opatoshu.) There were two poets living here, neither of whom had had much success, Isaac Berliner and Saul Glikowski. They were both in contact with Don Pablo Gonzalez Casanova, a philologist who my father admired a great deal. My father wrote his poetry in Russian, but following the Jewish rule that says that blessings are free when you don't have anything to eat, he decided to pray in the language that was closest to hand, or rather closest to the tongue.

'I started writing in Yiddish, because *beleiz breira*, I didn't have any other choice. If all I had was the blessing, because I didn't have the bread to eat, then I had to start eating in Yiddish.'

His first magazine was called *The Week (Die Voj)* and two issues came out, that is for two weeks. This magazine, which my father edited all by himself, was set up in Soledad Street, with Mr Biderman, who had arrived from Israel with someone else's wife: 'Our press was called *La Energia*, and all the energy was directed towards a little boy who died when he was only three.'

The press had a few Hebrew letters. At that time there were already about five thousand Jews in Mexico.

'Did you need publishing houses? Was there even a synagogue?'

'The first thing Jews do when they arrive in a new place is to establish a synagogue and a graveyard.'

The first Jew to be buried was a Sephardic Jew 'because none of the Ashkenazi Jews wanted to be buried.' The new Jewish cemetery was near Estrella Hill, and today it is opposite the British Hospital. I suggest that the name ought to be changed to Jews' Hill, so at least they could be associated with a place-name.

My father published his first real journal with Saul Glikowski, who died not long ago, and with Yosef Zajarias, who had been a textile worker in Bialostok and loved Jewish writing, especially works by Peretz, one of the three classic Yiddish writers (the other two are Sholem Aleichem and Mendele Meijesborim). Zajarias knew a lot about literature, because the workers attended the Hebrew University and read works by writers who were once very well-known in Poland.

The Jewish community in Mexico has always been small, but has always been very active culturally, with two daily papers *Der Weg (The Path)* and *Die Stime (The Voice)*. The first of these was founded by Moishe Rosenberg who died young and was then run by his wife, Sonia, with Jaime Ladesky, the senior editor. The second paper was founded and run for many years by its editor, Moishe Rubinstein, a great friend of my parents, who in the end died of cancer. There were also weekly publications in Spanish, *La Tribuna*

Israelita (The Jewish Tribune) and *La Prensa Israelita (The Jewish Press)*.

'I was the first to work on *Der Weg,* and I kept up my column for fifty years, until a little while ago, just a few months ago in fact. I was the first theatre critic in Mexico and I became a critic because the situation was critical (nobody was writing anything). I wrote parodies of things I didn't like and I was a big success.'

Sometimes my father wrote poems in Ukrainian, because he learned Russian later 'in the street' and at school where his Jewish teacher spoke nothing but Russian.

He published his first Mexico poem in Yiddish, in 1927. Before that he wrote one in the city of Ekaterinoslav (which was on the banks of the Dnieper and was later renamed Dnepropetrovsk by the Bolsheviks) that he showed to the poet Peretz Markish and to the poet Schmuel Halkin, 'a very peaceful, lyrical writer,' and I read him my first poem in Yiddish, which was entitled *The Oak Tree*. Markish said to me: 'Keep on eating and while you're eating, spit,' and Halkin wrote a few lines for me.

Until quite recently there was still a publishing house in Mexico that printed books in Hebrew. There was a typesetter who could set up the letters, though he didn't understand what they meant. The last book printed there was a collection of poems by my father, which came out in 1979.

While my father wrote his poems, my mother used to listen to them. It seems odd, but apparently all his poems were read out loud to her and she criticized them savagely. He used to accept her criticism 'with tears in my eyes'.

39

In 1964 my father and I went to New York, and during the trip he assailed my ears, which were already over-sensitive to changes in altitude, with the names of Russian poets. He might as well have been reading in non-alphabetical order from a telephone directory, and only recently, writing this book, have I been able to sort out some of those names in my own mind. In New York my father took me to the Jewish theatre to see a piece by the great poet Leivik. I could hardly understand anything, and I was reminded of how wretched I used to feel as a student, when I shot like a meteor through the firmament of the Jewish College without managing to learn any Yiddish. When the play ended we went on to congratulate the actors and I was behaving somewhat mulishly when a man came up, looking exactly like some of the men who I used to meet when I was little, and who used to praise me so effusively that I turned red with rage and embarrassment, only this man had an English accent. Then another one appeared who my father didn't know, but who said, 'Hello, Mr Carmel,' and my father was very touched by that.

I discovered later that in fact my parents' hidden reason for sending me to New York was so that I could marry the only son of a Mr London (an 'improvement' of his real name), a Jewish printer. He had made a fortune publishing Yiddish books by great writers who had fallen out of fashion. London had an office in Central Park which looked out over the park itself, *comme il faut*, where the walls were covered with valuable paintings, including some Picassos, Braques and Utrillos, but mainly works by great Jewish artists like Mane Katz and Marc Chagall. There were so many paintings hung on the walls that you could barely distinguish the work of one painter from another, though I remember a large blue Chagall. The problem was that the father liked me better than the son did. Alex was a dancer and very nice but he wanted to marry another dancer, whom his father didn't care for. My trip to New York was a disaster because I didn't get married and I didn't do enough shopping, and one evening, on 31 December to be precise, I had to walk twenty-five blocks in the freezing cold wearing shoes that were once wine coloured, with extremely high heels. I got blisters and felt considerable resentment against my father.

All this emerges because my mother recalls in glowing colours her magic time in New York:

'We were there in 1949–1950 for a reception at the PEN Club, because your father was a Jewish writer who was well known in Yiddish circles, and there are more people who speak and publish in Yiddish in New York than anywhere else, and they were very kind to him, and to me too, because in Mexico the Glantzes were in charge of things. We were invited to Leivik's house for dinner and his home made such an impression on me, it was so modest. There was very little furniture, a sofa made out of packing cases and a pretty plant and that was all. We saw him again in 1960, but he was very ill by then and in a wheelchair. He couldn't talk and we didn't know if he could understand what we said to him. Your father read his latest poems and he just smiled. His poverty, no that's not what I mean, his humility made such an impression on me, it was like Dostoievsky. I read recently that Leivik lived in a very old building on the ground floor, in a really gloomy place, very poor.

'Leivik's lack of money shocked me, nobody helped him to improve his lot, they all thought he was a good poet but nobody gave him any material help. Opatoshu was better off, he was a novelist and he wrote articles for magazines. One day when we were visiting he told us he was frustrated because he was writing a very important book and he had to hunt around for subjects for his articles. He asked me for suggestions. He was a very good friend, he published the first two cantos of your father's poem "Columbus" in his periodical *Zamlung (Miscellany)*. I've got a lot of his papers, I ought to sort them out and give them to a museum, nobody else will if we don't. I wrote to him from Trinidad ... have you been to Trinidad? ... it's a lovely place, and he sent me a card back which read: "You've had enough beauty, now go home." You girls were on your own. He was a friend, a real friend.

'I met his wife Adela when I was with father in New York. She was a very well-dressed woman, very refined. We had dinner at a French restaurant.

'Yes, she was very refined. I don't want to sound nasty, but all the poets had wives who were anything but humble women. She was very dynamic. She lived in an apartment and rented a room because she didn't have enough money to live on. Opatoshu couldn't change things by then, he died very suddenly, he was only about sixty-four or sixty-eight. They had one son, David, who was an actor.'

'Yes, he made a lot of films, I saw him on TV just the other day.'

'They went through a lot because of him. He married a Yiddish girl, but then they divorced. Once he came to the restaurant half in rags and he said to me in Yiddish, laughing: "Luci, there's a *boziak* here." '

'What does *boziak* mean?'

'*Boziak* means tramp in Russian.'

'She killed herself, didn't she?'

'Yes, she was very lonely.'

40

A few weeks ago Morris Brown died. Along with Morris Gelber and their wives Rosa and Genia they were a solid bastion of Mexican Yiddish theatre. If Jewish writers in Prague (or so Kafka says in his *Diaries*) could complain about the lack of interest shown by the Prague Jewish community, whatever can be said of a Jewish community that has steadily lost its attachment to ancient traditions in the Yiddish language? I've often looked without looking at the many photos of people who appeared alongside my father, almost always taken by Martin Ortiz, a photographer who lived at Madero Street, and who mean nothing at all to

My parents (top left and far right) with some Yiddish players

me. Now I recognize with some emotion that many of them were poets, others were famous actors who travelled the world, but who never received the acclaim given to classical performers though they were stars of the Mexican Jewish theatre which survived more or less unchanged from 1925 to 1960.

'In the daytime they all did other things, but they came together in the evenings to rehearse and watch plays. There was Malka and Fanny Rabel's mother, Betty Rabinovich, she came from a family of actors, the Kompaneietz, who used to travel around Russia and Poland (and Berlin, too, I imagine, where they would stay in the Immanuelkirchstrasse where Felice Bauer lived when she was receiving instructions from Kafka to go and see the work of his friend Lowy at the theatre). Betty was born on the boards, she was only six years old when she first started to act.

'About twenty years ago the committee of Pioneer

Women (a Zionist organization of which my mother was a member) organized a celebration of her sixty years in the theatre. She's about ninety now, but she's still bright and alert, she lives with Fanny.'

'Yes, and Malka became an actress too,' says father.

'Now she's a theatre critic, that explains it,' I say.

'When they had the celebration, all the actors living in Mexico joined in: for example, there was a Polish lady who must also be about ninety, Pola Patroni, whose husband was the leading Yiddish theatre director in Poland. She's quite a lady,' reflects mother sadly, 'but now I never see her at all.'

The Mexican Jewish community was small, and doesn't bear comparison with New York, nor even with Rio de Janeiro or Buenos Aires. What prompts Jews in exile to cultivate this sort of theatre? Is it nostalgia for a land that never belonged to them, but that was somehow definitely theirs? Or is it the creation of a sacred place, somewhere they know well, where just for a moment they can exist because it's staged for them alone? Or is it because the expression of the faces or sound of the voices makes them quiver with a sense of recognition? The fact is that everybody goes to the theatre, the theatres are full. Which ones? The one they rented, the Abreu theatre, and later on the one they owned, at Leandro Valle. Perhaps the theatre explains this need that so many Jews have of submerging themselves in a totally Yiddish world in order to understand themselves, like when lots of young people used to go to my mother's house (when she barely knew Yiddish, though she did know Russian). For instance Mr Lisker (who is nearly ninety now), the brother of one of my parents' best friends who died in a fire at his paint shop, and whose wife Clara used to come and visit us when we were little. She always brought us a present, and I still remember those ritual presents, not because of what she brought, which I have completely forgotten, but because of the act of offering. Would it be chocolates or cakes or a toy? I don't know, because it didn't matter, it just stays in my memory with the rustly, crunchy feel of the wonderful wrapping paper.

Another thing strikes me and makes me think. Most of the actors came from performing families, and when the parents had a child it went into the theatre, and those children, like circus children, started out on a curious double life, travelling and performing, and the performing led inevitably to marriage within the theatre and so the whole troupe were joined in life and on the stage. Kafka talks about the Tschissiks, a funny unpronouncable name to us. My parents remember the Rabinoviches, the Patronis, Leon and Tzilia Zuckerberger, the Guinters, Niura Eizengord and Yidl Epstein who performed his own play.

'Was it ever published?'

'No, in those days people were . . . there were promoters too, I remember Chesa Gurfinkel especially, he's still alive, he must be about eighty.'

Sigmund Turk came once, that extraordinary actor who later founded the Wikt theatre in Israel. I remember him, he had a powerful way of looking, and there was a kind of light around his head and his eyes, a light that still shines out of the photo where he is with my parents, and with the beautiful woman who was his partner on and off the stage.

'Lots of actors came here. There was Morris Schwartz, for example, another great actor.'

'And Berta Singerman too,' I say, adding a name.

'Yes, but she was nothing to do with Yiddish theatre, she performed in Spanish.'

I remember Berta Singerman well, I even saw her perform in the Palacio de Bellas Artes. My sister Lilly saw her several times, when I was still very small, and she was so impressed by her appearance and her voice that afterwards she became the family's official actress, the infant prodigy who recited party pieces on all special occasions.

'I met Hanna Rovina in Israel, she was the great Jewish actress who worked in the Habima theatre, and who had worked with Stanislavsky; she did The Dybbuk for him, you

know, that means when someone is possessed by a spirit ...
possessed by devils, she performed plays by Ibsen and
Dostoievsky's *Crime and Punishment*, *The Mother* by
Gorky, and she died in February 1980,' says mother.

'I published plays in Odessa. I wrote *Ruined Worlds* and
Snow in Springtime.'

My mother's voice chimes in again: 'That theatre was
very strange to me, because I was used to Russian theatre
and the Odessa opera.'

'The community were all young, and spoke only Yiddish
and they performed *Tebie der Miljiker (Tebie the Milkman)*
here and *The Dybbuk* by Ansky. I've already told you that
the Jews always set up a synagogue and a school, and here
we set up various journals where I wrote pieces on theatre
and lots of other things, all sorts of pieces, for fifty years
non-stop. And we set up a theatre too.'

'Where are your plays now?'

'Here.'

And he pulls out a cloth-covered book, an exercise book
written in Yiddish with a quill pen, and his initials J.G. on
the cover. My mother has tidied it up. Mother takes out two
bulky volumes, the *History of Yiddish Theatre*, which tells
of Kafka's friend Lowy, and Hanna Rovina, Sigmund Turk
and a lot of others, including Malka and Fanny Rabel's
parents and my father too. The book was written by Zalman
Zilberzweig.

41

A pause here: I look round and notice that my story has
turned into a portrait gallery and that other characters have
appeared from what my parents have said. Now there is a
Nobel Prizewinner, Isaac Bashevis Singer, who my father
saw several times in New York when he was living in the
Bronx, near another friend of theirs who was a poet. My

father went to his house quite a few times, and always thought he was reserved, distant and even hostile.

His other brother attracted attention, the one who emigrated to the United States much sooner, about the same time as Opatoshu in the early years of this century. He was called Israel Joshua Singer, author of *The Brothers Ashkenazi* and a famous short story, 'Pearls', and several plays. Isaac arrived in 1936, a writer like his brother, and added the name of his mother Batsheva to his own name, since when he has been known as Isaac Bashevis Singer. Both brothers published in *The Yiddisher Forwerts*, but only the name of the elder was mentioned, and the one who won the Nobel Prize does not even feature in Jewish encyclopedias of the 1950s.

'I was staying with him in the same hotel in Tel Aviv, and I got to know him really well. We used to have breakfast and all other meals together. My first impression of him was that he was a man who didn't know how to handle people at all, but I soon changed my mind about that. He was very intelligent and very warm-hearted, but a bit shy and he was a vegetarian (like Kafka) and he used to keep quiet a lot, though he was always very friendly with me. We went out together down Ben Yehuda Street and I didn't notice a step and I fell down and cut my head open. He picked me up and took me to hospital, and then he waited ten hours for me until they discharged me. He must be about eighty-five now, and his brother must be about ninety-five if he's still alive.'

'When did that happen?'

'Don't you remember? 1972, the year there was an exhibition of my paintings in Copenhagen. As a result of that fall in Tel Aviv I developed a blood clot and had to stay in hospital more than two months. Maybe you forgot about that?'

'Don't let's talk about dismal things,' says Lucia interrupting. 'I remember in Israel, when we were there in 1955, that Scholem Asch came. Do you know who he is? Scholem

Asch. You'd met him before, hadn't you?' she says, turning to my father.

'I used to see a lot of him in New York, we had long talks and I went round to his house.'

'In 1955 there was a celebration for him in Miami, organized by Catholic ladies on account of his book *Mary and the Nazarene*. There was a big debate about it in Jewish circles, and everybody was furious because they thought it was a betrayal. When he went to live in Israel everybody saw him as a blasphemer. They welcomed him very differently, I can tell you. We were there with a friend of ours, David Zakai from *Davar*, the most important Hebrew journal in Israel, and he'd been told to go and meet Scholem Asch and he asked us to go with him to the airport. Asch was really well-known then, his book was a bestseller and had been translated into several languages, and when he saw the miserable reception laid on for him, with just three people, he got really angry. I don't quite know how to convey this in Spanish,' says my mother getting worked up, 'but as I said, it was a very humble welcoming party. He was a tall, good-looking man, very distinguished and stately and he must have been about seventy then, he died in 1957. I looked at that great writer who was so furious with his fellow-countrymen and fellow-writers, who must have all been jealous of his success because he's dared to write in a new way. He walked into the airport building with his head held high.'

42

Everyone who emigrates to America thinks he's another Columbus and the ones who go to Mexico want to be like Cortes. My father preferred Columbus and, like the Cuban writer Carpentier he wrote an epic-lyric poem about the Genovese explorer. In between writing verses he pulled out back teeth. He had his dental surgery on Seminario Street, number 10, and he had bought a place belonging to Dr Olivenski who went to Israel and died out there. It was a nice enough surgery, with three rooms, a waiting room, a laboratory and what might properly be described as a consulting room. He had an assistant in dental technology, Dr Marienstrauss ('a handsome young man, very well-turned out, a Viennese'), and there they undertook all sorts of small technical jobs in between dealing with the patients. My father performed ten to fifteen extractions every day. He was paid three pesos a tooth, but 'all the blood was revolting'.

He began studying dentistry while he was selling bread. he thought it might turn out to be an easy profession, useful as a way of earning a living and a lot quicker and easier than medicine, 'though I was wrong,' it might have been better to have studied medicine because dentistry was 'a bit mechanical' and dull. In between one tooth and another he built crowns and wrote a lot more poetry. He also worked in the Beistegui Street Hospital sometimes and my sister Lilly and I used to go and see him and play at pulling teeth out.

'I did hardly any fillings because that was too boring.'

Pulling teeth out was less boring but a lot bloodier. The one thing that mattered to him was reading and writing poetry. In 1936, he wrote 'Blood-stained Flags', a political poem in honour of the Republican forces in the Spanish Civil War, and then two years later he wrote his poem dedicated to Columbus. He had been collecting material on Columbus and just needed something to trigger off his muse. That something happened as a result of a visit by the principal critic of Yiddish writing in New York, Dr Samuel Nigger, who deliberately used such a pseudonym in a country where there was discrimination against negroes. His real name was Tchorne, which means black in Russian. My father read him his Yiddish poems and agreed that he would not write on contemporary subjects but would concentrate on the history of Spanish Jews expelled from Spain

MARGO GLANTZ

at the same time as Columbus began his voyage of discovery.

'He said to me: That's what you ought to be writing about, nobody else knows as much about that period as you do. He stayed five or six days in Mexico and I wrote the first two parts of my poem in just four days. I used to read it to him every day and he was very enthusiastic about it. He took some parts with him to publish in the journal he ran in New York, *Zaml Bijer*, along with the poet Leivik and the novelist Opatoshu. That's where my poems came out, and they were considered very important in the Jewish literary world.'

Nigger went by ship and returned to New York via Havana.

'He wrote to me on that trip that Columbus was with him.'

According to Nigger, my father made a big mistake with 'Blood-stained Flags' becaue he wrote about something contemporary, something that was going on at the time, even though he had written some good poems. And with his Columbus 'I made another massive mistake: I dedicated it to Nigger because he had inspired me to write it and so I tied his hands, he couldn't write freely about my work. That Columbus poem earned me a big name in Yiddish literary circles internationally, I stepped up in a big way. I wrote "Kzaid Erd" ("Piece of Earth") afterwards, and that also appeared in the New York journal.'

Kzaid is the piece of bread that is torn off the loaf before the Sabbath blessing. Later he wrote another great poem, 'Nizaion' ('Trial'), dedicated to me when I betrayed the chosen people. I appear like a black sheep in that work, but at some point, I don't know when, I turned into the Prodigal Daughter.

There is no such thing as a race without its own cooking. Or even without its daily bread. That's what Bernal Diaz meant when he described the tortilla as 'the corn bread that they make'. I know it by heart, and I could almost say that flour runs in my veins, though flour from another sack, from Carmel, where they made little chocolate rolls shaped like coffins, sweetened with nuts and soaked in a liqueur that might have been cognac or rum. I used to call them ecstasies. I don't cry; I just don't remember anything else.

My mother is the same. She sold Carmel, yet still she goes on making those typical dishes that all my sisters except me can make. They all know how to make Hebrew and Yiddish golubtzes (minced meat, raisins, cabbage, tomato and a pinch of sugar) and Lilly can even make the Russian ones, because they were the best and my parents barely knew any Spanish and hadn't (still hadn't) decided to hide in that cuisine. They knew how to cook gefilte fish, very difficult to prepare, about as difficult, apparently, as Mexican molé (spicy, hot sauce), before they packed it in jars, just as nowadays you pack Manizevich, stuffed fish, in the United States where it goes straight from the jar to the plate. In Mexico if you want to eat gefilte fish the way my aunts Mira and Jane used to make it, you have to eat with my sisters or my mother.

'How do you do it, mother?'

'I can still remember, though it's a long time since I made it, it doesn't agree with me. Old Consuelo used to be very good at making it in the restaurant, and then Rosa was good too. Now let's see if I can remember: you mince your fish, either sole or cod (or both), yes, both, and you add minced onion, diced carrot, salt and pepper and beaten egg. I never put bread in mine, but some people do. You have to decide how much you're going to need and then you put it in a pan with fishbones, fishhead, the skin, some onion and add water.'

'And garlic?'

'No, no garlic.'

'Really? I thought it tasted of garlic.'

'No, not garlic, sliced onion, sliced carrot and a pinch of sugar.' (All Jewish cooking has a pinch of sugar in it.)

'You boil it all until it turns to jelly, about twenty minutes, then you take it off the heat or you put it on an open flame like fish rissoles and carry on cooking it slowly for another two hours. And that's it, all you need to do is spice it and add your own salt and pepper. I'm not very good at it myself, it's over twenty-five years since I last made it. Lilly can make it very well, though I didn't much like the way she did it yesterday.'

'But you make really good *holodietz*, mother. Now tell me how to make that.'

'Well, you can make it with cow's feet, but I make it with chicken feet, gizzard, wings and the chicken's carcass, and the neck. You boil them up with a bit of salt and some onion until it's all starting to disintegrate. Then you take out all the bones and strain the broth, making sure you don't get any onion in it. You strain it all, and then mince a bit of garlic, add some salt and boil it with a little chicken jelly, just a little, and then cool it and that's all there is to it. The hard part is taking out all the little bones.'

'And how do you make vareniques?'

'Oh, Margo, I've a lot to do, leave me in peace.'

'Go on, tell me, don't be mean.'

'You can stuff the pastry with different fillings, minced meat or chicken. You make them with some fried onion and chicken fat. Sometimes they're made with kasha. You make your pastry with flour, egg, a bit of water and a little bit of salt to taste and that's it. Your sister Susana has a recipe in a book, ask her for it. That gives you all the instructions.'

'Now I swear this is the last question. What about *gribelaj*?'

'You make *gribelaj* with chicken fat. You put pieces of the fat in a pan with a pinch of salt, and when it starts to turn

My mother (left) and aunts, 1928

golden you put in the onion and fry it for a few minutes, then you take out your *gribelaj* and eat them right away.'

44

Once Carmel was in the Zona Rosa, right in the centre of things. The sculptor Matias Goeritz, recently arrived in Mexico, went there and met a Jew with a beard who was messing about on a typewriter, a Jewish model with a carriage that went from right to left. Jacob used to write with his thumbs, his elbows and his beard. Goeritz watched him in amazement and from that back to front beginning there developed a friendship which was definitely the right way round and which still continues to this day. Arreola, the writer, went there too, before he appeared on television and set up literary, cake-eating Saturday meetings. Pita Amor, the poet, made her reappearance there, loaded down with bracelets and jewels and wearing a percale dress that had seen better days and was full of holes.

'Dozens of intellectuals used to come to Carmel, but Matias Goeritz was one of the nicest, he was such a good man, a really fine person,' says my mother.

'Goeritz used to inspire me and he pushed me to work, to paint and sculpt. He was a born modernist, a man always looking for new forms. I worked on my bits and pieces because he forced me to, and that's how I came to exhibit in the garden of the Museum of Modern Art. The main pieces were Totem, The Annunciation and Not Noah's Ark.'

'Yes, Pita Amor, she came in with all her jewels and her clothes in rags. She said: "How are you, señora Glantz?" and then all of a sudden a cat walked in and there was such a fuss, Pita was screaming and so were the waitresses and they they all started laughing. She was as brazen as they come.'

'She was so beautiful when she was young, but then she

ended up like that . . .'

'Half mad because of you.'

My mother is still jealous, and since I know what jealousy feels like from my own youth, I reserve judgement on the subject.

A gallery was set up in Carmel.

'My first exhibitors were Manuel Felguerez and Lilia Carrillo. She was very much a realist painter, I've even got some of her paintings from that period.'

'What was Felguerez like?'

'He was very young, a sculptor mainly, he didn't really paint much then and his wife was a realist painter,' my father says once again.

A lot of names are mentioned, including Omar Rayo and Leonel Gongora, both from Colombia.

'They exhibited here too, they were good friends of mine, especially Leonel, who started to paint seriously and used to come out in the summer with Vita Georgi, who he was married to at that time. He painted my portrait and gave me a lot of pictures. He was very talented. Vita used to paint as well, Gongora favoured a sort of exaggerated eroticism, he's a painter with solid realistic, satirical roots, you might describe him as a neo-realist or even a super-realist.

'And there was Guillermo Silva Santamaria's group. He was Colombian too, a famous engraver, and he took part in the exhibitions held at Carmel and ate cakes there with all the others.'

'That was a very promising group.'

'What about Corzas?'

'Corzas had work on show here too. He didn't live in the real world very much, but his paintings were real enough. He came with Bianca, he was very clever and he was a realist too.'

Vlady left a mural in Carmel, depicting my father as a scapegoat.

'Vlady was a friend of mine for many years. I knew his father, Victor Serge. Vlady and I shared a good friendship, the same language and the shirt off our backs. We always spoke Russian together. We'd had a very similar education. Isabel, his wife, even worked with me too, when I set up the Glantz Gallery in Genova Street, above the patisserie.'

My mother interrupts. 'Ludwig Margules lost his slim figure at Carmel. Every Saturday after the theatre he'd come in about midnight and ask for *cholnt*, that's a typical Jewish dish: tripe stuffed with flour and fat and meat, with pearl barley and French beans.'

'Yes,' smiles Jacob, 'you leave it in the oven all night. That's why we like it so much, you put it in at night and take it out in the morning.'

45

All my family knew Elias Breeskin, friend of Jascha Heifetz. 'He was very rich to start off with, he earned fantastic money on the radio,' said my brother-in-law Abel Eisenberg, the musician.

I remember him in the Czardas where he was playing the violin while people ate sausages. My mother remembers him in Cuba Street, in a Jewish club where my father worked when times were hard.

'Your father was working there as a . . . an administrator, and Breeskin came in, a huge man in a black overcoat, as though he were lost, and he asked me for a loan and I don't think I gave it him, and he just collapsed, right there, and fell through a glass panel. Just imagine! He was such a big man.'

'Did he faint or what?'

'I don't know if he fainted, or if he was drunk. He used to drink pretty heavily.'

'Sometimes he'd come out to Carmel and say: "Yasha, will you stand me a meal?" And so we'd feed him. He was a millionaire and then he started gambling and ended up in jail with gaming debts.'

'He passed cheques that bounced.'

'He was married to a Jewish girl and they had three children. She left him afterwards, I'm sure she couldn't stand the way he was going on. He married again and had two children, Olga who was a chubby girl, and a little boy, and they both played the violin.'

'He was a great musician, and the President got him out of jail.'

The conversation is taking place round the table, after a family meal. Everybody is talking, you can't tell one voice from another.

'So Olga was chubby, was she?'

'Well, when I knew her she was as flat as a pancake.'

'The violin settled her down. She's a wealthy woman these days.'

'He was an amazing musician.'

'He was a friend of Heifetz. Once Umansky, the ambassador, invited him to the Russian embassy to play chamber music.'

'Umansky was a lovely man, so well-educated, but he was killed, you know.'

'Yes, a bomb on his plane.'

'Breeskin was an extraordinary performer, I'd say he was virtually as good as Heifetz.'

'No, nobody was that good.'

'I met him at the Faculty of Letters,' says Lilly suddenly.

'Who? Heifetz?'

'No, Henry Szering. He was with Amalia Hernandez.'

'I met Heifetz in Odessa,' says mother brightly. 'He used to live opposite our house, I'd see him from my window when I was studying, and I saw him and his mother going for his lesson.'

'Fancy that! His teacher was Zagurski, the character Babel wrote about.'

'No,' says Abel, 'he wasn't. His teacher was Misha Auer, he taught all the best violinists, people like Misha Ellman and

Ephraim Zimbalist and Heifetz.'

'And Menuhin?'

'No, Menuhin was born in California. No, it wasn't Misha Auer, it was actually Leopold Auer, Misha was a famous North American film actor.'

'Then Zagurski must have been inspired by Auer, because Babel says that a lot of children studied music with him, and his special talent was bowing.'

'Heifetz always used to wear a sailor shirt and navy blue trousers,' says mother. 'He started touring when he was only eleven years old, and he used to go round with his father because he was so young. His parents were simple middle class people. My father was friendly with the priest from the orthodox church and my brothers used to go out on their bikes with his children. Jews were on good terms with priests, sometimes they even intermarried.'

'Does Heifetz still play?'

'No, he has arthritis.'

'Do you want any fruit?'

'I've just had some, thanks.'

'How tragic, for that to happen to a musician!'

'Two spoons? Three! that's bad for you!'

'The percussionist was very nice. Luyando was his name, he played with the Mexican National Orchestra, he was in charge of the staff.'

'We knew Milstein very well.'

'I knew him from Odessa,' father interrupts. 'I went to see him here when he gave a concert and he said: "Where have you sprung from?" We were good friends.'

'Yes,' says Lilly, blushing. 'Now I'll tell you something I've never told anyone before. And don't be cross. When Milstein came over I was about twenty-one and one night he invited us to the cinema — you, father, Abel and me.'

'Was I there? I wasn't even in Mexico?'

'Well, we all sat down and Milstein started doing this . . . stroking my thigh and I tried to move his hand and in the end I gave him a slap, and he was furious and got up and left.

When the lights came on again Dad asked me where Milstein was. "How should I know?" I said. He was very good-looking and a real ladies' man, like Rubinstein. He was in the same room as Abel and he kept looking at himself in the mirror all the time and combing his hair.'

46

Proverbs don't last forever. My father spices them up a bit. He takes the well-known one 'A horse gets fat if its master just looks at it' and adds 'but the master gets thinner', a useful clue to understanding why our fortunes had such ups and downs. I have already said that my parents went from job to job, though they occasionally stayed in one place long enough to over-eat or try on shoes. The repeated occasions on which food took a central role ended in disaster: they had a little café on Guatemala, a side street, although my father kept going to other cafés and restaurants, especially cafés where the literary groups of that now-vanished Mexican society used to assemble.

The café on Guatemala was abandoned in a power cut, I gather, because during the cut my father took a little oil lamp and set fire to the place. I may be exaggerating, but among all the burned things there is a leather purse that my mother was given by her brothers on her fifteenth birthday, a purse with her name engraved in gold and which is now in an old photo album with ivory covers belonging to my younger sister, Shulamis. Everything remains in the family, except that first café which later on, in 1954, was turned in the Genova Coffee Shop. That was where my father first had to deal with the problems of his art gallery and began to show works by painters who were not very well known in those days. He showed muralists, naturally, then he moved on at Carmel to the newer artists. He began selling bread very early and his persistence in supporting us all lasted through many years. In between, there were neckties, a lot of paper, steel combs (to delouse us during the changes from school to school) and moves through a series of homes, that feeling of permanent exile, all the unpleasant surprises, maybe as far back as the games we used to play at Chapultepec, where we were lifted up onto horses or mules. (The horses used to throw us and demolish the Amazonian image we used to try to cultivate, with our sailor hats that used to fly off at the stroke of a whip. I should explain: the whips were nothing to do with the horses, they were just part of our game, and my father used to ride with us — there were only two of us sisters then — on those absurd equestrian dodgems.)

The bread stayed warm and so did the teeth when they were pulled out of mouths. Carmel became associated with elaborate cakes, Viennese cakes or those apple cakes called strudl. My mother had learnt how to make them when young, and immediately they were transformed into a means of making money. Then came nut rolls and on the side Felguerez decorated the new gallery with ships' ropes, since some of his first works were on show there. A lot of writers used to go there when times were hard. Juan de la Cabada had a charge account in the restaurant and used to eat there when he didn't have enough money to go anywhere else, while my father went round all the tables answering the needs of the Americans who used to come looking for kosher style Mexican food. There are always reminders of the stuffed fish or manna transformed into soup that were eaten during the celebration of religious festivals in my aunts' houses, those two red-haired aunts who came to Mexico via Constantinople, bringing in their luggage those huge necklaces of red amber that I used as marbles when I was small. Sometimes there would be borscht and *golubtzes*, with black pudding or with meat.

My mother's recollections sometimes involve princes (not all that charming), and those princes lived in Mexico, like prince Yuri Dolgoruki, a member of Czar Nicholas's family. He used to eat blintzes in the Carmel restaurant often enough, and besides being a prince he was well-educated and intelligent.

'Because some princes are complete idiots.'

Prince Dolgoruki was (moderately) rich and left everything he had to a French priest who used to work in the English Hospital consoling Catholic patients, and occasionally orthodox ones too, such as a White Russian prince, a relative of a Russian engineer, who was also a nobleman, but who didn't have either the nobility or the sense of humour of a Nabokov or a Dolgoruki.

'The Dolgoruki estates are all in ruins in Russia; the *kolhoses*, the peasants, left the land, as happens everywhere else, and went to live in the big cities, so the old provincial estates all collapsed, and the Dolgorukis were no exception. I read that here,' says mother, looking up from a Russian magazine. 'This is the oldest journal in the United States to publish in Russian, the *Novoia Ruskaia Slova (New Russian Word)*.'

'Yes, in Pilnyak's novel *Mahogany*, the antiquarians, the Bezdetov brothers used to live in Moscow, in Dolgorukova Street, which used to be called the Street of the Abattoirs,' I tell her.

'Fancy, I never knew that ...'

You can find all sorts of princely remains in Paris, and until quite recently it was not unusual to call a taxi and find that the driver is a duke or a count fallen on hard times. Even I have my princes in this democratic age with overthrown Shahs and all the rest, and once when I was standing in a queue outside the Bibliothèque Nationale in Paris (where I was engaged in research on exoticism) I heard a porter say:

'Attendez, mademoiselle, vous êtes en train de faire la queue avec un véritable prince.'

Naturally, I showed the patience of a saint while the prince got tired of waiting in the boring queue.

My mother also remembers a Hindu prince who used to visit. Tall and stately, with a finely chiselled face, he used to bring us sweets (that was when my father was a dentist, so we weren't afraid of tooth decay). His name was Bezra and he appeared on Sundays, the day when everybody met at our house to have tea with strawberry jam and home-made biscuits. Bezra used to come to our house when my sister Lilly was two (I still wasn't born or else I was snuggled in a crib, swaddled in a kind of embroidered shawl which left only my face peeping out). We had a maid called Rufina, who the bricklayers called Rufina the whore, a name that my sister repeated with precision and some delicacy. Bezra laughed and talked to my father who later decided that the profession of anthropologist better suited him than dentistry, though the latter was certainly the profession that enabled us to entertain more people on Sundays. Besides the blintzes, Prince Dolgoruki used to love fish soup, a Russian dish that my mother used to make as a substitute for caviar.

Later on, the painter Fernando Leal used to visit, the man who painted frescoes. My youngest sister Shulamis was born by then, and he asked my father if he could borrow her as a model for one of his angels. My mother refused, afraid he might hang her up to fly and she might fall down, but I suspect that was just a way of avoiding him paying court to my sister Lilly, who was fourteen years old by then and looked dangerously like Veronica Lake.

The Sundays continued and the house stayed full. I think my parents realized that it was more practical to run a café, and so they set up Carmel.

48

Marc Chagall was in his nineties and still flew over rooftops, as his paintings show. Occasionally he would go on one of those trips with my parents, because fate sets things in motion from the very beginning. My father's native village was called Novy Vitebsk, and that village was the overspill from Vitebsk, the village where Chagall was born, a hamlet of wooden houses and *servas* (Russian churches) with village synagogues, one of those tiny places full of impoverished Jews with beards.

'Some people think old age is the end of the world,' says my father, 'rather like those birds that cross the marshes without getting dirty.' He's talking about Chagall, who he met in Mexico in the early forties, through Diego Rivera who introduced him to Chagall in a letter, written on 13 August 1942:

> Although I regret not having the pleasure of meeting you face to face, I am taking the liberty of sending you another letter. My friend, Jacob Glantz, the writer (he is a poet and an art critic) and editor of the Mexican *Jewish Gazette* would very much like to interview you on behalf of his readers. This is the reason why I have burdened you yet again with a letter. I am most grateful for any assistance that you might be able to give my friend Glantz.
>
> I hope you are enjoying life here. I shall look forward to meeting you shortly, and in the meantime send you all my good wishes.

And that led to another repeated pattern. My father went to the Bellas Artes and watched the painter coming and going. He retraced the same steps he had climbed with Orozco, Rivera and Fernando Leal. Now he visited him every day in his studio in the Bellas Artes, where he was scrambling up steps to design the choreography of Diaghilev's ballet *Aleko*, which was based on Alexander Pushkin's *Gypsies*.

Bela, 'his inspiration,' was there too, the woman who acted as model in so many of his famous paintings, such as 'The Bride Dressed in White', 'The Wedding', and 'The Burial'.

'He was always asking her what she thought.'

'Chagall was very friendly,' says mother, 'very nice, and his first wife Bela, who he had lived with most of his life was a charming woman. They got to know each other when they were young, and when he went off to study away from Vitebsk, she stayed in Russia in further education.'

The Chagalls stayed a little while in Mexico City in the 1940s, and they used to visit my parents and have tea and blintzes with them. Bela used to read her poems and stories, including one called 'Fiery Veils', after the oil lamps that used to be lit in winter on Friday nights.

'I must look for a book.'

And by a stroke of unexpected good luck he finds it along with another one too, a book in Yiddish called *The First Meeting* and the other, translated into Swedish, *With Love*: they are both written by Bela Chagall.

He saw Chagall again in Saint Paul de Vence in 1964.

My father called Chagall from Paris. Chagall's comment was: 'Get in a car and come and see me.' 'How can I do that if I'm in Paris?' 'Well, take a train then.'

When my father got to the station, Chagall's chauffeur, a White Russian aristocrat, was waiting.

'There was a beautiful park with horses round his house. He had lots of paintings that he refused to sell.'

And just to confirm the law that everything comes round more than once, my father went into the shrine and watched the painter at work in his studio.

'He never let anybody in when he was working, but he let me in. I didn't realize then how important it was to be painted by him.'

My mother interrupts:

'You always realize things like that afterwards.'

49

Kafka's mother remembered her grandfather who died when she was six years old. She remembered how she had touched him and kissed his swollen toes, asking his pardon for things she had done that might have offended him.

Chagall seeks pardon in my father's recollections.

My parents went to New York to see their great friend Yosef Opatoshu the novelist, who was very close to the Chagalls. Bela had died and Chagall appeared. He said: 'I committed a sin.'

On another occasion, we are sitting round the table before tea and sponge cakes. We're talking about Bela, who wrote short stories that Chagall illustrated. We're talking about this minor poet, and my father translates a few lines:

You, poor soul, weighted down with tears
neither stars nor clouds pass before us.
Once upon a time in the sand
Moses died . . .

'Do you know his present wife?'

'Yes, she's a hideous fat old Russian woman.'

'Is she Jewish?' I ask naively.

'Obviously! Chagall only ever married Jewish women.'

'What?' interrupts Mother. 'That's not true.'

That was his sin.

'Chagall's only daughter (there are three grandchildren) hired a housekeeper to look after her father when Bela died.'

'She was an English nanny, all shrivelled and faded and dried-up, a really unfortunate woman, and then suddenly they got married.'

They had a son.

Everybody gossips in the Opatoshu's home. Chagall is a lot older than his new wife.

'Then things started to go wrong,' says my mother.

And the daughter got angry, the wife stood up in a rage and started shouting that the boy wasn't Chagall's.

'Since then, nobody has ever mentioned her again. Complete silence. She doesn't even have a name.'

'But she was called Virginia,' says mother triumphantly. 'When Opatoshu called us at the hotel and asked us to go and see him, he said: "Marc Chagall's coming over with his new wife, Virginia." '

He had painted her as a figure of adoration, worshipping the baby, the child who may or may not have been his.

'Bela died in the Opatoshu's summer home, just outside New York.'

'No, she died in France, she had a sudden heart attack and died.'

'No, she didn't. It wasn't a heart attack at all, she had angina and she died when she couldn't get her breath.'

Despite the different versions, her death was real enough. Bela disappears and in the space between her going and the arrival of Valia, 'an aristocratic wife,' the Englishwoman who doesn't even merit a name, came and went again.

My parents were in Israel in 1952. My mother only stayed just over two weeks and in Jerusalem she went to a little café called Kasith (The Cabin) where a lot of painters and bohemians (*beheimes*, Jacob would say, which means 'animals' in Hebrew) used to gather. The talk was all about Chagall and his wives, with particular attention given to the Englishwoman, 'the shadow that even he can't remember, that he never mentions, he only ever talks about Bela and Valia.'

The painters talk happily about the scandal in all its detail.

'He never forgave her, she insulted him too deeply and in public too. That was his punishment all right. For his sin.'

Poor Chagall never had the chance to obtain forgiveness from Bela's swollen toes, since I don't think he ever painted them.

50

Murals are part of Mexican history. And you can't have important murals without frescoes, which date from early colonial times. When you go through Huejotzingo on your way to Cuautitlan, you pass the Jewish Club, where there is a mural by Fanny Rabel, and the Acapulco Street synagogue where there is a mural by Arnold Belkin, in defiance of Jewish law which forbids the making of graven images.

That law was broken under the close watch of a rabbi, señor Maizel, an important member of the community and Jacob Glantz. The possible interpretations are legion; as many as are allowable according to the Cabala. Belkin is in despair at the conflicting opinions of his advisors: my father takes him on one side and says:

'Which one of us is doing the painting? Aren't you the artist? Then go ahead and paint what you like because otherwise you'll end up not painting anything. Don't tell the others I said that and get on with your work.' Vlady also paints a mural at Carmel. It is on wood and is reminiscent of Chagall at times, for example when my father climbs onto his scapegoat as an act of contrition, in an obsessive, symbolic position since his beard has always been rather like that of all goats everywhere.

Jacob suddenly starts writing poems in Spanish. 'He's a Spanish poet now.' He recites them to some of his poet friends. Then he collects nuts, mirrors, trumpets, trinkets, old clocks, paintings from the market, blowlamps, screws, and he works scrap iron into sculptures that sometimes appear in biennial exhibitions, he even imitates the painters who sit eating enchiladas or kreplaj, and paintings by important painters begin to disappear from the walls, and the walls begin to be covered by countless paintings full of faces, with distinct expressions, luridly coloured and decidedly autobiographical. The painters are pleased with him because every time they go in, he has created a pictorial history of them all which he hangs in chronological order. In a little while Carmel has run out of painters and is transformed into a shrine to the narcissism of one who has transgressed the law by spreading graven images. Glantz is the rabbi or scapegoat, it doesn't matter which. His face shines out in cobalt blue, sepias, reds, and one crimson eye moves behind him, while another is earth coloured, his mouth is yellow. He shows them in the Bellas Artes.

The paintings alternate with portraits and Gongora paints him as Toulouse-Lautrec's double. In front of the paintings nightmares and racial prejudice are discussed.

'Dad, what does racism mean to you?'

'I'll tell you. When I was visiting some African countries, where racism just goes on and on as though nothing had happened on that continent, I started noticing the differences in people's skin colours and once I asked one of the local councillors a question. My friend, who was also a very fine lawyer, said this to me: "I'll show you the extent of the problem by telling you a true story: a coloured man was on trial for killing a white man and stealing his horse. Since the crime had been committed within the boundaries of states X and Z, the judge allowed the man to choose which law he wanted to be tried under. 'I choose the law of state X,' said the man. 'Fine,' said the judge, 'you'll have to pay five pounds for the theft of the horse and we'll hang you for murder.' 'Just a minute. In that case I'd rather be tried under the law of state Z.' 'In which case you'll be fined five pounds for the murder and hanged for stealing the horse,' replied the judge."'

51

They say that memory 'leads back to itself' and maybe that's also true so far as things forgotten are concerned. There may be repeated memories, reshaped five or six times in the mind and each time differently, like those multiple stories about the death of Miguel Paramo, the famous Mexican hero. The bread basket stays the same, and so do the teeth that eat that bread, bread and teeth travelling together and constantly present in all the versions. Between 1925 and 1930 my parents tried a whole range of business ventures, though they kept the bread-selling going throughout. Then all of a sudden Uncle Volodia appeared and joined my parents in the enterprise called Apollo, either a stationers in Jesus Maria Street, just to be different, or perhaps a cardboard box factory: memory can't quite stretch so far as to clarify that. There was a restaurant too, in what is now Guatemala Street opposite the cathedral, next to one of those shops selling religious artefacts. There are even a few combs, handy for combing dolls' hair, that passed through our childhood, leaving their imprint, in particular leaving a scar on my sister Lilly's hand. Some old gloves in a style that quickly became fashionable mark the crucial stage when we ran a hat shop and my sister Lilly began to go out into the world on her own, getting onto buses and trams with her three tickets (that cost 25 cents), which gave her as much prestige as Jane, Tarzan's Jane that is. Such adventures were forbidden me, and just thinking about them was as far-fetched as crossing the ocean in a caravel, maybe even on the *Santa Maria*, which set sail on one of the shelves loaded with sculptures that my father had had made for his study. Above, on the other side was an oil painting of Columbus stepping onto American soil (that got lost in one of our many moves). Next to it was a painting of father, dressed like an artist in a reddish silk dressing gown with an abstract design on it, painted by Ignacio Rosas. In between there was a juice stand from 16th September Street, where they used to give me mango juice. Then a harsher image, the attack on my father amid metres and metres of black- and white-checked woollen cloth that we used to make baby clothes, and that still comes in handy for daughters and grandchildren. My mother set up a shoe shop and ran it, though before she had run a restaurant.

'How did you feel about running a restaurant?'

'It was like going to jail. I felt the same with the shoe shop, it was so lonely, in such a poor district and I didn't know a thing about shoes, nor about shop-keeping. I couldn't even change buttons or buckles.'

My mother sells shoes, my father sells bread. Memory shifts about, is overwhelmed by forgetfulness, is linked to questions of identity, turns itself round.

Returning from his travels around Latin America, my father decides to set up another restaurant and does so in the newly developing Zona Rosa district, alongside Montecasino, where for the first time bread and fishes come together under the same roof, poetry meets the coffee shop, the sound of spoons mingles with the sound of words, words which are now coming out of a tape-recorder, sentences that don't quite fit together, monologues that dissolve.

'I bought a shoe shop and a cakeshop. Later it became the Genova Coffee Shop, I was the first one to set up a restaurant with chairs and tables outside in the street, a pretty little restaurant and I opened it with an exhibition of paintings by Rivera and Orozco.'

'How did you manage that?'

'I was good friends with Rivera.'

'Where did you meet Rivera?'

'Here in Mexico, I went looking for him.'

'What did you say when you found him: I'm a Jewish poet and I'd like to get to know you?'

'No, we talked in Russian, which he spoke very well, though with a strong foreign accent.'

One of my mother's friends met my uncle Benia in Odessa and told him that my mother ran a restaurant. He couldn't figure it out and next day he turned up again carrying a tiny little cake in his hand:

'Does she sell this kind of cake?'

My mother used to play the piano in Russia.

52

One of the simplest artistic devices is repetition. Which is what I've always experienced. Sometimes numbers appear that signify moments in my early childhood. We go past streets and houses that I can hardly remember at all now. We lived on Amsterdam and Atlixco Streets, on the corner of Michoacan, and on Atlixco Street on the corner of Juanacatlan (which doesn't exist any more, swept away in the urge for change that constantly reshapes our lives). My parents knew Capuchinas Street before it was given the pompous name of Venustiano Carranza. I've lived through all sorts of changes: San Juan de Letran and Niño Perdido are now known as the Lazaro Cardenas Boulevard. I knew La Piedad before it was renamed Cuauhtemoc. I just hope La Merced keeps its Jesuses and its Marias, its Correos Mayores with Eden and its Suns and Queens. And I hope nobody thinks I've anything against great patriotic heroes, including Don Lazaro who nationalized the oil fields.

My sisters and I were given a variety of elegant names. First and foremost, we were flowers rather than girls: Lirio (Iris), Margarita (Daisy) and Azucena (Lily).

'Why did you give us names like that?'

'Because Jews usually name their children after dead relatives, and I wanted to give you poetic names instead.'

My youngest sister was the only one who was named after her ancestors: Shulamith, who was named after Solomon's beloved. Her name was a combination of the names of both our dead grandparents: Mikail, my mother's father and Sheine, my father's mother. Death is rounded off with flowers.

I never liked my name. There are dozens of Margaritas in literature: Marguerite Gautier, Margarita Ledesma, Margarita esta linda la mar ... Margarita Glantz, Margarita ... I hum a line from the tango ... 'You're not my Margarita any more, you're just a Margo now ...' Besides, whenever anyone calls me Margarita, I feel that it's followed by a snarl, and the gradual pulling apart of my petals as someone intones 'She loves me, she loves me not' in their heads. I don't think I like that sort of thing. The poetic nature of my name and my sisters' names means that we're always mixed up when it comes to legal matters or official registers, apart from the fact that they usually list us ten years out of date. Poor Azucena — no, Lirio too — has had to suffer the burden of a name that is so flowery that every time she goes through the process of writing it down for posterity, posterity appeals. I don't believe that anyone can proceed into posterity with the unfaded name of a flower cut in the distant innocence of childhood.

My father smiles. All that matters to him is his beard, which is turning grey and thinning out. And the marvellous freedom he has enjoyed in this country, from the very moment he set foot here, the very moment that he decided to stay on the boat to Veracruz with the advice and money loaned him by the captain of the Dutch ship.

Now he starts reciting something in a low voice. He's still smiling and he suddenly says a lot of words that sound splendid and are all jumbled together. I listen to those words as you might watch somebody crying, without understanding anything, because he is speaking in Russian. Every time he does this it lasts a bit longer. Now he backtracks and recites in Spanish the first poem he wrote when he arrived in Mexico:

> . . . my brothers live across
> the street in the United States.
> I come from a street that does not
> have a name,
> Where every year there was
> a fair
> and a pogrom.

53

Down in the Gulf of Campeche, in a dusty little street in the village of Tacuba, water is very scarce. Teams of men of all ages load small oriental-type flasks and take them round from house to house. In those days I used to set my hair — or rather it was set for me — with lemon and sugar water, with little fringes round my head and a sort of bunch in the middle. I couldn't say my emms, I used to make them sound like vees, and the neighbourhood kids used to make fun of me and shout 'Hey, Vargo' and I used to cry. My father fell ill with pneumonia at that time and stayed months in bed, and instead of giving him penicillin, they used to put glass things on his shoulders — cupping glasses is the term I want — which would sink into his skin and make a vacuum. When you took them off they made a popping sound and I used to think how great it would be to have pneumonia. I would stand in the doorway and watch, and he would get annoyed and one day he threw a slipper at me, which hit me on the shoulder.

'I was ill when they gave a party for me when my book *Blood-stained Flags* came out, written in honour of the Republican forces in the Spanish Civil War. I made a speech. It was a restaurant in Avenida Juarez, and then I left very abruptly and caught cold. I was six weeks in bed and then they sent me off to Cuernavaca where I stayed three months in a *pension*. I was being looked after by Dr Ulfelder.'

Dr Ulfelder also delivered babies and helped at the birth of my sister Susana in the American Hospital, which was in the Santa Maria district. Later on it amalgamated with the English Hospital. That's where Dr Ulfelder took out my father's appendix.

'He did a lousy operation on me, the wound wouldn't heal and I don't know how I managed to recover. I was three weeks without moving at all, in a room with three other patients. One was an Arab and he kept saying "Allah! Allah!" all the time.'

One of the other patients was an Arab Jew and the other was probably Mexican. Then he was allowed out in the garden during the next few weeks. Finally he was allowed home, whereupon he moved to San Lucas Street, to a nice little house in a tiny square. Lungs identify or trace one's destiny. Mother had weak lungs and when she was a girl, around 1915 or 1916, they sent her to Dr Kransfeld's sanatorium, more of a holiday home for Jewish children with lung defects. She went through the long ritualized treatments with the rest of them for just three weeks, the sort of treatments you can read about in *The Magic Mountain*: eating, sunbathing, resting on chairs facing the mountains, going back to eat again and finally the miraculous recovery. Sanatoria for tubercular patients in Russia were called 'white flowers', no doubt with half a thought for the white camellias worn by the languid, but intelligent Alphonsine Plessis, afterwards known as Marie Duplessis, countess of Perregaux, Dame aux Camélias.

Later on, my mother was studying medicine and the same Dr Kransfeld taught her specialist subject: the respiratory tract. Some of her school mates were royal princes. It was snowing and people were hungry, it was after the revolution, in 1922:

'I went out of the house padded up with all the clothes I had and I went with some of my friends to the doctor's house, because it was so cold in the university and the lecture rooms were so big it was impossible to keep still.'

The doctor gave a lecture, explained how the lungs worked and when the students started to get tired, he didn't offer them the traditional cup of tea, he didn't even light the samovar, he just played his pianola.

54

For a long time I used to think that the Argentinian fascination for science fiction or fantasy writing could be explained in literary terms, the sort of explanation that involves discussion of sentence units, semantics, narrators.

Possibly one could follow Borges's line of argument that all fantastic writing is a branch of metaphysics. But I think the real explanation is a lot simpler and less logical: Argentina is a country whose passion for telephones has not been satisfied for the past twenty-two or twenty-five years, so that any aspect of day-to-day reality turns out to be completely fantastical. I'm going into all this because my destiny was predetermined by the fates (as opposed to the fairy godmothers of the type that helped Sleeping Beauty out), and that destiny was not only responsible for my being a wandering Jew going from home to home (all those removals of my childhood!), but it also made me a pupil in a variety of schools in different places. In particular, there was the Argentine Republic School, where I started in the fourth year of primary school, a crucial year in my development because I learned to sing both the Argentine national anthem ('Hear, oh ye mortals, the holy cry of Liberty, Liberty, Liberty!') and the Mexican anthem ('Oh, the daring . . .') Those anthems always started the week, on Monday mornings at precisely eight o'clock. Every line of the anthems brings tears to my eyes, because when I was very small my mother passed on the habit, (or rather her own tendency to cry) and so whenever I hear a national anthem I start to cry myself. Yet ironically I can't wear contact lenses because I don't have enough moisture in my eyes and my corneas get blisters if I try. I was talking about my fantastical destiny that began with moving from house to house and was briefly anchored for a decisive period in that brother country of the Southern Cone. In fact, I could well have been an Argentine citizen, a Jewish gaucha or portena. My grandparents thought about going to Argentina in 1915, but my grandmother decided to stay in Russia, because she thought that she wouldn't be able to find any servants if they moved, and as a reward for that she got caught up in the revolution. My parents favoured the United States, but now here we are in Mexico. Poetic justice is fantastic too, and now the children of my mother's cousins, who emigrated to Buenos Aires, live in Mexico for a particular reason: that is, for the same reason that forced quite a number of Argentinians to move here. However, whatever the explanation, the fact is that I have ended up in Mexico and since I was born in this country I don't have an Argentine accent, which can sometimes cause problems. Still, I have strong links with that country which seems to have pursued me all my life, even when I was in Paris, where I helped some friends who afterwards became Peronists to take a portrait of Peron out of the Argentine House at the Paris university campus. Then I was involved with the Fondo de Cultura Economica in Argentina at a time when it was run by the nicest editor in Latin America. I talk about these things, people tell me I'm antediluvian and I try to reassure them that I'm not so old, it's just that I'm Jewish and in the Bible years are doubled. My relationship with Argentina still continues: I have a daughter who is half Argentinian and I'm completely in love with the tango, I keep singing: 'You're not my Margarita any more, you're just a Margo now.'

55

Twice in my life I've felt like Columbus (my father wrote an epic poem in Yiddish on the great Genoese sailor and everything stays in the family). The first time was when I went to the Near East with Paco Lopez Camara, and we only had one scholarship between the two of us and I preferred to buy earrings in the market in Cairo and Damascus and Istanbul instead of buying food, and I ended up with an attack of scurvy. The other time was when I first went across the Verrazzano bridge in New York, and I never have been able to pronounce 'e' and 'i' in English properly, so the American police couldn't understand me at all. Fortunately, all I had to say was 'bridge' and not 'sheet', because it's so

The ship brethren, 1925

easy to make a mistake like a small child and slide from sheet to shit, which is where linguistic confusions start, along with international diplomatic incidents. Still, all you need to know is that twice in my life I've felt like Columbus, without actually knowing for sure whether I was sailing in the *Niña*, the *Pinta* or the *Santa Maria* or anything else for that matter.

In all sincerity, as they say in Colombia, all women have something of the Columbus in them. We all have to tackle the question of which came first, the chicken or the egg, and long before Columbus we all had to resolve that famous placentary riddle for ourselves . . . We've all had to sort out, in our heads or elsewhere, what that split between chicken and egg might mean, and then we've had to put the two together in our writing. That's why we go on travelling, because in earlier times we would have had to go out surrounded by our escorts, wreathed in high ruffs or dressed up as men like George Sand or Shakespeare's Rosalind.

Going back to Columbus, I think the difference between

us at least is my lack of avarice, since in spite of the great distances he sailed when he counted the range of languages spoken and birds flying round, he was always able to show greedy enthusiasm for gold, no matter how thin or base it may have been and when he was dying he could still announce: 'Gold is magnificent. Gold is the basis of all treasure and anyone who can get enough of it can do what he likes in this world and retire to the Kingdom of He who assigns souls to Paradise.' At least, that is what Ramon Iglesias wrote in his *Columbus the Man*, one of the many books that was listed in the bibliography that my father drew upon in writing his great poem 'Columbus', which has only partly been translated into Spanish, by the Colombian poet Leopoldo Rosas, who changed its style somewhat. My father says that I should have translated it, but I don't know Yiddish, except a few words relating to food and shouting at people. My travels have been much more modest, and instead of hunting for gold my long journeys across this continent (during which I've acquired a few figs, some llamas, a small piece of patchwork and a rather modest precious stone with a flaw in it) have been retracing the steps my father once trod.

56

Sometimes getting round Mexico City involves long journeying. You might chose to go down to Ermita Iztapalapa highway, down Viga, keep on going a long way and then turn down R. Gomez highway and after passing all sorts of multinational factories, eventually you get to the Free University of Iztapalapa and almost feel like Cortes. I feel like a female version, burning my boats or turning them round, when I finally turn my car onto the highway that is still under construction, with bits of paper and cans between the barriers — a sort of repetition of the huge tracts of waste ground that you see in cities such as Newark in the United States.

I find a hall, rather than a theatre, and a queue of young people (though they shouldn't be crowding round like that if they want to queue seriously!) is building up around the tiny little doorway and I prepare to listen to the National Jazz Competition, organized by the Cultural Office. We wait half an hour overwhelmed by whistling, tape recorders and cigar smoke, and we notice the ash being dropped on the brand-new carpet in the hall (and I tell myself, regretfully, that young people just don't care, and after all I'm the only woman of reasonable age in the whole place). The judges finally arrive, after a wild journey through the surrounding neighbourhood. The sound system starts working (badly) then everything settles down and a group of eight or ten young men start playing a kind of jazz somewhere between cool, to start off with, and dixieland later. Renata asks me: 'What sort of jazz are they playing?' and I answer 'Mixed jazz', and every time a group appears I say the same thing, even when they are playing bossanova, until finally she says: 'I thought you were supposed to know something about jazz.'

Eventually my family's turn comes round, and yes, it really is my family because there is my daughter Alina on piano and Ariel, my nephew, on saxophone and harmonica; Salvador, (my son-in-law) with his beautiful tangled hair on violin; Jacob, a young Brazilian who looks like a carbon copy of Salvador, on guitar; Andres, a family friend also on guitar; and Jazzmoart is on drums and paints abstracts on the walls. I think it's all wonderful and smile at people round me who look at me as if I were an idiot and my stomach aches as though I'd eaten something that disagreed with me and then I watch Juan(ito) (I've always called him Juanito since he was tiny) striding up to take the mike and saying that people say there are no jazz groups in Mexico and now here there are a good thirty-three. And the height of the microphone forces him to stoop over, changing our perception of his size, in much the same way as the great size of Mexico was drastically reduced when somebody went off and discovered the Indian sites that were later conquered by Cortes.

When Om (my family's group) finishes playing, Renata asks me again: 'Is that mixed jazz?' and I don't deny it is. We go out, or rather we try to, since getting out of the hall involves pushing through a great crowd of young men all listening with rapt attention, and I run into some friends and throw my arms round them and ask them all sorts of family questions and since I try to get out as soon as Om has stopped playing, I meet up with my tribe out in the corridor, I fling myself on them and start kissing them wildly on cheeks, beards (if they have one) and foreheads, until finally one of them pushes me off and I retreat. Renata complains that nobody is paying any attention to her at all, and we leave, setting off from Iztapalapa on our journey homewards to Coyocan, with visions of the festival floating up at us out of the smog.

57

Now Christmas is approaching. It's time to celebrate the posadas, the stages of the Virgin's journey to Bethlehem. Once they used to do this properly, back in my childhood in Jesus Maria street, in that enormous house where there were forty flowerpots in the patio and thirty-eight piñatas (great hanging pots filled with all sorts of things). My uncle Volodia has recently arrived from Russia and had joined in the processions and gone on to break piñatas. My uncle was very good-looking, a mixture of the man of marble before he turns into a statue and the outsider who appears in the Itzvan Szabo film. My Oedipus complexes started with men who looked like my uncle. Adults and children all joined in the procession and candles were lit in the great patio, we all chanted the litany and we felt like Joseph, or more especially like the Virgin Mary.

'I was really frightened,' says Lilly, 'I thought all those candles might start a fire and when the children started driving out witches with fireworks I was terrified.'

The piñatas were filled with peanuts, limes, sugar cane, oranges and candy. Some of them were filled with powdered tomato and some with ashes. They were all fantastic shapes and when you knocked one down, it was like bringing down the whole world. My uncle Volodia invariably hit the one with the ashes or the tomato, and he always used to look at us in an aggrieved manner, covered in ash.

The lady who shared the house with us was named Chonita Cervantes, and she had a proper shrine with figures of saints and another one with German porcelain dolls, which had wonderful eyes and used to sit in rows on little chairs beside tin beds with embroidered covers. She used to give us little baskets with sweets and prickly pear juice in a dining room with Tiffany lampshades and leaded windows. It was almost as nice as our first Communion, when we wore white silk dresses and carried white leather bound missals, and ate tamales and had fruit drinks, and found *Christian Martyrs* in a printed edition beside our plates, and other wonderful books which my father forbade us to read, but which we read in secret, so that afterwards we could go and confess our sins, terrible sins that could only be purified with four, even forty Ave Marias, a hundred Credos and a few Paternosters. Confessing and taking communion were as entertaining as reading dirty books or listening to tangos.

Later on we lived in Tacuba and a friend of ours had a little house that you could get to by tram, near the house of Goyo Cardenas, the Mexican Jack the Ripper. That meant that we could go round the gardens and see the holes that had been the graves of all the poor wretches killed off by the evil chemist. My friend's name was Bertita and she was very fond of her food, or rather her mother was, and maybe she wasn't even my friend, but my sister Lilly's friend. What I do remember clearly is that one day I left home to go and play with Bertita who had a collection of paper dolls and dresses (which were also German, it was just before the period of all the persecutions, maybe even during them) and I used to dream about having a collection like that if Bertita died: that's when I felt like following the example set by Goyo Cárdenas; I was six.

Then we moved to Amsterdam Street, Shulamis was born and in the apartment next door someone had left some photograph albums with pictures of Greta Garbo, Carole Lombard, Bette Davis, Gary Cooper, Clark Gable, Claudette Colbert, Charles Boyer, Marlene Dietrich, John Barrymore, Barbara Stanwyck, Cary Grant and Don Ameche, and my happiness was so complete (as was Lilly's) that I forgot all about my murderous instincts towards Bertita, though they transferred onto my younger sister Shulamis. Sometimes I scalded her, without meaning to, with her feeding bottle and then I had to sing songs to make up for it. Lilly had taken over all the photos of my favourite stars and the children were skating in the patio.

When I was thirteen I went on a train for the first time from the big square to Tacuba. I sat next to the window and a man put his hand on my thigh, and I piled my books on his hand and we travelled on like that until I stood up and rang the bell, with my face burning as though I were running a high fever. My mother had taken me to Armand's, in Palma Street, to buy material for a birthday dress. I chose a Paris model in a magazine called *For You*, it was blue and had a bolero and a collar with geometric patterns on it. The neighbourhood dressmaker made the outfit for me, the one whose nephew was called Julio and who Shulamis called Culo (Arse), which upset the child who told on her to my parents. The dress and the child stay with me. Afterwards my mother and I went all round looking for shoes to match the dress. I got a pair from our own shoe shop, and I got a slap into the bargain from my mother, after she had shown infinite patience ritualistically going round to see the neighbours who, of course, were all Jewish.

It rained in torrents at Tacuba and the mud smelled terrible. We used to be carried shoulder high down the street, but we were a lot smaller then, during our first stay in Tacuba, before Shulamis was born, when the smell of mud mingled with the gorgeous scent of night-flowering jasmine and the barking of our dog, The General.

58

My real childhood spanned the whole period when General Cardenas was in power. When I started in my very first year of school we were living in a village in Tacuba. I learned to read without knowing I was doing so; the way you might look at rain or just walk and the only prize I ever won in my life was given to me in the Francisco Eduardo Tresguerras primary school, a block away from our house. I don't know if the school stayed or moved somewhere else, but it doesn't matter, what I remember is a great big patio and I can remember the headteacher, señorita Baliaquí. She was very fond of me and my sister Lilly because we used to take turns at wearing the same cat-fur overcoat or cape that looked expensive and rather elegant. We wore it because classes began in February and it was very cold in the mornings. I still feel nostalgic when I recall those mornings when we used to walk straight to school at half past seven, with red noses and hands covered in chilblains. The city was soft and almost transparent, it would be icy cold and the sun used to glisten on the mountains. There were hardly any cars, just hordes of children walking to school on their own.

The militaristic sound of the name Tresguerras (Three Wars) set the tone of the place, and we used to have to sing loudly every morning, with the implacable cruelty of a socialist education policy: 'young guard, young guard, do not give them, do not give them, the cruel, implacable bourgeoisie, do not give them peace or quarter, peace or quarter.' I never did find out who Tresguerras was.

I was talking about the prize I won. The only one in my whole life. Well, they gave it to me because I learned to read without any help from anyone, probably just by looking at all the books on my father's shelves. My prize was a little celluloid doll with artificial hair shaped round her face in a 1920s style. It was a talking doll. It had a peculiar little machine in its belly with strange round bits that all looked exactly alike, and the whole thing was carefully held on with sticky tape. Out of those round bits, from behind the sticky tape, came strange deep sounds like a ventriloquist makes. I was so fascinated by the mechanism that I wanted to take it to pieces. I took the doll home and that night, when Paula our maid put us in the old tin bath, heated by a wood-burning stove, that night I started on the doll which never uttered another sound afterwards. My punishment for that has been never ever winning a prize again. After that I wandered round like the Holy Virgin of Gamboa, from place to place and from school to school. Sometimes we didn't even stay in the same place more than two or three months, with the result that for a while I was struck dumb by it all. I snapped out of that pre-psychological dream when I heard the notes of the Young Guard song.

My first contact with petrol was through my hair. I often used to get lice, an unavoidable feature of state education. In the afternoons my mother used to wash our hair with amethyst-coloured petrol which left us smelling terrible and with sore eyes. It might have happened on 18 March 1938, the day the General took over the oilfields. After that we had to start combing our hair with special nit combs and Paula used to enjoy herself as the bugs fell out. I can still hear the sharp crack of a louse being crushed between our maid's fingernails and the rather sensual but not very cheerful feeling of having a comb dragged through my hair and across my skull. Then when we were cleaned up and the lice had all been killed off and the nits all crushed to death, my mother would rinse our hair with powdered stone and vinegar and then for a grand finale she would put lemon juice on us and give me a fringe and tie up a little bunch of hair on the top of my head. As the lemon juice dried, my hair would set like stone, as unmovable and unshakable as the buildings in the city of Celaya.

We used to cook on coal stoves and we had no running water. We bought our water from the water sellers who went up and down the streets shouting their wares. Our house in the Gulf of Campeche had a square patio and a little garden with night-flowering jasmine and two dogs. I used to buy chocolates with cherries in them at El Paraíso. It was the most wonderful place imaginable, full of glass jars with sweets and chocolates in every conceivable colour. My sister Lilly liked large round blocks of chocolate which had hollow centres and were filled with liquid toffee. They cost twenty-five cents, the same as the cherry-filled chocolates. We used to run down the street counting Cadillacs, and then we would climb up the legs of the gigantic statue on one of the foutains which you can hardly see at all now because there are so many cars in the streets.

Besides the Young Guard I can remember figures from illustrations in *Blood-Stained Flags*, which my father had written in Yiddish. The only thing I could understand was the illustrations. There was a picture of two workers, pretty much like other pictures that were around at the time. They were wearing light-coloured clothes and across their shoulders was a red and black banner which read: 'No pasaran!' That phrase has stayed with me too: 'No pasaran! No pasaran!' along with 'Do not give them peace or quarter.'

I can remember the General's voice. Sometimes I think it gets mixed up with some of the tear-jerking soap operas I used to listen to in my childhood, when for some reason or other I would have stayed off school, and out of the wonderfully shaped radio would come tangos or songs by Maria Luisa Landin or the General making speeches or some announcements.

Sometimes there would be jokes in circulation: 'There goes old Big Mouth' and we'd say 'Where?' and look up and see the General with his big, fat lips going past.

My hatred for Fascists was only softened by my love for Christian martyrs, along with sweet tamales, and I used to pay my respects to them (through books) thanks to those kind, well-intentioned families who had taken the trouble to save me from the pangs of hell. I was about nine years old then. My First Communion was a landmark on the road between the socialist workers and the Christian martyrs.

I also remember the children of Morelia, children who had been evacuated from the Spanish Civil War. We used to study together. They all had something in common with the General, who had been brought up religious and then turned to socialism. Their lives were very similar to the lives of the neglected children in my favourite books. One of those children seemed like Oliver Twist to me, or the orphan from *The Mysteries of Paris* or Esmeralda from *The Hunchback of Notre Dame*, books which I read later. I remember that some of those children went on to university with me, and they seemed to be living out scenes from books about neglected children. Life provided them with a decent future, just like the characters in the novels.

My hatred for Franco was fuelled by the evacuated children, my father's poetry and the General's speeches.

59

It may seem rather excessive to say that I've known Catullus, of all people, intimately since I was girl. But I really did know him, through reading an anthology of classical poetry that my father had somewhere on his oddly assorted bookshelves.

My parents were bilingual, and they would use their

MARGO GLANTZ

knowledge of two languages as a defensive screen, something secret and special that I could never be part of, except
for my inordinate passion for Dostoievsky and the discovery, later on in my adolescence, that I belonged (in some
third corner of myself) to that Russian soul which could
kneel down in a public square and confess out loud to the
wind, as Raskolnikov did once (with very negative reper-
cussions) and as I am doing now in these pages.

So I read Catullus, and Leopardi too, who have something
in common, their lameness, despite the distance in time
that separates them. The range and disorganization of my
father's books reminded me of the Tower of Babel; alongside
Dante there was a book by Vargas Vila or a pamphlet by
Ponson de Terrail. Then there was an edition of Laurel
which got lost somewhere in the house, probably loaned
out to a friend (or stolen), Pablo Neruda's poems and next to
the Bible a study of Neruda by Amado Alonso, and several
blue-covered volumes of *Florilegio*, published in Barcelona
by the Cervantes Press in 1936. *Florilegio* was an anthology
of great poems in Greek, Latin, and Portuguese translated
into verse by Fernando Maristany, with three prologues and
some prefaces. I learnt many of the poems by heart, and was
able to use them whenever I lost my keys or broke a doll.
Ariosto and Pietro Bembo went with me in between reading
Jules Verne and listening to the *Tango Hour* (with Carlitos
Gardel, Azucena Maizani and Rosita Quiroga), together
with a few cherry chocolates that my sister would go and
buy for me in the shop on the corner called El Paraíso,
provided I promised to give her the silver paper.

Ariosto says: 'How beautiful you are, my lady,' and Gardel
recalls, 'Twenty years are nothing,' repeating, 'Do you
remember, brother, what times we had, twenty-five Aprils
past?' and I start crying miserably, even though at that age I
hadn't even seen twenty-five Aprils. I was such a precocious
reader, and in those days there were Indians who used to
carry little girls so their shoes wouldn't get muddy and I
would be reading John Dos Passos, or listening to Tchai-

kovsky's *Francesca da Rimini* or Mozart's *Rondo alla Turca*, imagining some lover calling to me, in spite of my poor sense of geography. At that time, no it must have been quite a lot earlier, my father was working on a journal entitled *Ruta*, a literary tower of Babel, with contributors from all over the world. Those were the best years in the city, when Don Lazaro ran things, after the take-over of the oil-fields.

60

When I was sixteen one of my elder cousins got married, I think it was Lila. At that time it was fashionable to wear knee-length black dresses, as Chanel dictated, covered with sequins, really eye-catching. I'm not trying to insist on how shiny the dresses were because that must be obvious, but my sequins were brighter than anybody else's and outshone even my sister's. Mine were Mexican pink and hers were dark blue. Even dressed like that I didn't manage to entice any of the young Orthodox Jewish men to dance with me. Lilly, on the other hand, kept whirling past like a spinning top (I think that's the right image). I was totally obsessed by what I looked like (I should add that my hair was always wild and had acquired a rough, tough texture that made me look like the famous freefall wrestling champion Blakaman) and when I paused to reflect that someone was bound to come and fulfil my lofty and rather sullen desires, the well-known Jewish musician Don Moishe Ivker struck up a tango on his violin.

Jewish weddings were celebrated in the Nidjei Israel, in Justo Sierra Street, in the first synagogue built by the Ashkenazi community. When I heard the tango my heart swelled and the sound of the accordion joined in like a knife through butter and I sat there without moving, admiring the way my dress glittered.

The same thing happened to me when I was a Zionist —

A Jewish wedding in Mexico, 1932

or rather when I joined a Zionist group. (Young Jews were socialists and revolutionaries and, moreover, less given to differences.) After the serious indoctrination sessions there was dancing, and everything was fine when we danced the hora but when we started dancing in pairs I was left on my own. At least that was a slight change; before I never even got off my chair. Then I remember a trip I took with my sister Lilly to Patzcuaro, with the children from the Israelite College, children who were not like us at all, because we had always gone to non-Jewish schools.

In the evenings there were talks in Yiddish and I had to go along, sitting there, half listening, ready to perk up again at the sound of applause. Once I heard someone say something that made my ears prick up, just as those tangos of my adolescence had done: 'That Glantz is such a brilliant man, it's a shame he has such stupid daughters.' I forgot to say that my father had come to visit us and one night he had made a very witty, passionate speech that everyone had applauded wildly, apart from me, because I fell asleep half way through. I console myself with the knowledge that there are music critics who fall asleep half way through the Ninth Symphony and don't even wake up with the Ode to Joy. It was during that trip that we heard on the radio about the bombing of Pearl Harbor in 1941.

I attended the Israelite College for two years (and hated every minute), where I took special courses and argued with the teachers who tried to treat us like Polish or Ukrainian kids back home even though we were in Mexico. They had all come from Europe, they were refugees who didn't speak Spanish and we would use all sorts of dirty words that either drifted over their heads or were filtered through Jewish phrases. Once a new headteacher came, the pride of the anti-zionist socialist movement, and he asked me if I had read *Tebie der Miljiker*, Sholem Aleichem's best known play which had been transformed into *Fiddler on the Roof* on Broadway. I said no with some difficulty (he didn't know Spanish and I had hardly any Yiddish) and he asked me how it was possible that the daughter of a Jewish poet had never read that play. I still remember how ashamed I felt, especially since his question turned out to be prophetic and I married outside the chosen people, like the Fiddler's daughter. She ends up regretting it (because her husband leaves her after saying all sorts of terrible things about her Jewish background), though that didn't happen to me. My parents were very hurt when I married a goy, but they took comfort when they learned that thanks to the grace of Providence my husband had been circumcised when he was born and had something of the Messiah about him. Now my father takes it quite calmly when some young gentile asks him to act as godfather at a late circumcision, performed to enable a Jewish girl with orthodox parents to enter into the state of holy matrimony.

61

Travelling used to take a long time. You would set off by train, then transfer to a ship. Cases would be piled up like houses, huge trunks with all a family's belongings, all their memories, sepia coloured photographs, goose feather quilts and mattresses, cupping glasses, those little crystal vases that sucked out infections. There would also be little suede shoes from a boutique (of which there were still a few left in Odessa) that cost a million roubles. Here in Mexico the most expensive shoes cost six pesos and had cut leather work, bows and little heels. Every time my father caught anything, those cupping glasses would be ready, they just had to be warmed with alcohol and inserted into the skin which would greedily suck them in. Sometimes poultices were used too.

When the Second World War ended my father got a job in a relief organization for displaced Jews and every time we went to meet him at the airport (the airport in those days was just a big shack) I would know that my destiny was to travel, like Telemachus who roamed the universe in search of the fame his father had enjoyed. Dreams of that future travelling used to end when I saw my father's suitcases, as he came back from Guatemala with embroidered handbags, or from Panama with a rubber bag which would be fashionable today, or from Venezuela or Brazil with dried flowers, or from Peru with little silver llamas or bracelets made of coins that my sisters wanted desperately.

My mother travelled a lot too. In this respect she is quite different from Penelope, and she never set about large weaving projects to deceive her suitors. On the contrary, we went off to the United States to buy clothes to sell on the black market. In my bedroom there are still tailored suits in several sizes bought on Fifth Avenue, the colours of which have hardly faded at all. They were grey with vertical stripes in beige or green with bright red, or mustard with coffee brown or cocoa brown with burnt sienna. Very few suits got sold and we were always wearing them. They were very elegant and nicely cut, like the ones that Humphrey Bogart wore when he played gangster parts, and my sister Lilly looked dangerously like a film actress, both in the way she did her hair and her colouring. With a bit of effort she could look like Lauren Bacall, which made me green with envy. The suits were a huge success with us, but a failure with our customers. I don't think my parents had much taste in shops, and certainly they didn't in cloth, because time and again there was always a lot of material left over to be recycled. I particularly remember a certain kind of check woollen cloth (also very good quality) which belonged to a time in my distant childhood when they used to make winter clothes European style, with black velvet collars, all neat, classical and very proper. Later on pinafore dresses came into fashion, in the days when blouses were puff-sleeved and after that came tailored suits with belts and shoulder pads, and then Dior suits which were loose-fitting and long waisted and were worn with narrow patent leather belts. Styles changed, but the cloth stayed the same.

Once I went with my mother on a trip to Dallas. It was oppressively hot, but the white women were still dressed elegantly. I remember a tall, very tall blonde woman with enormously high heels and a huge straw hat à la Greta Garbo. We went by Greyhound bus from San Antonio to Dallas, and I was going to sit at the back of the bus and the driver said that 'nice young ladies' shouldn't sit next to negroes. When we went back to Mexico, we took a second class bus from Laredo to Monterey, which was a completely different experience: we were travelling with chickens. Nobody tried to stop me sitting with the hens, in that situation of democracy and underdevelopment. After that we travelled in a train without air conditioning. I slept next to my mother in a top berth, wearing a violet Chanel suit. You can learn a lot from travelling.

62

Every day I go down the street now renamed after Miguel Angel de Quevedo, an early ecologist known as the Apostle of the tree. Miguel Angel de Quevedo would turn in his grave if he could see that the tallest of the Mexican cypress trees that used to grow along the narrow, beautiful avenue have been torn up and destroyed. Now the remaining trees will be isolated and their roots (that you can see through the soil) will be crushed by the yellowish pavement and by all the heavy trucks that pass over them, with the result that the trees will lose their colours and the rest of us our clean air. I can't feel any satisfaction when I go down Zamora Street in Coyoacan which has been virtually disembowelled for some months now because they are laying huge pipes inside its delicate belly. Even the drunks in the El Combate bar are upset about that!

Still, I suppose we should console ourselves. Lima is pretty horrible too, and streets are being destroyed in Buenos Aires, and art nouveau buildings are being torn down in Montevideo, though those countries are all further down the road to underdevelopment. Even Caracas has traffic jams and buildings are replacing trees and the mountains are disappearing from the horizon, though that seems impossible, since Venezuela has only just become an oil rich nation and we have all kinds of natural resources here in Mexico.

Nevertheless, I can't do anything but sink back into nostalgic recollection whenever I go into a museum and see up on a wall a painting, sometimes a huge one, by Velasco, and I am faced with the former crystalline magnificence of this region. There is an almost epic quality to the light.

My real inner passion reaches the limits of its survival when I read José Emilio Pacheco's *Las batallas en el desierto (Battles in the Desert)*. And of course when José Emilio starts that first chapter with an archaeological title 'The ancient world' and that world doesn't even stretch as far as the excavations of the Great Temple, then you can understand the great age of just Miguel Angel de Quevedo's trees and accept the possibility of their destruction.

I go on travelling through his pages and I see that when José Emilio was little there were already supermarkets and I make comparisons: when I was little I lived in Tacuba market which used to flood every day in the rainy season, which was practically all the year round, and I used to listen to the radio, or rather station XEW when my mother didn't have anyone to leave my younger sister with, and so I would stay at home and miss primary school (which was compulsory). I used to travel (I have to admit that I am older than José Emilio) with Flash Gordon out to Mongo but I didn't realize that my childhood was unusual, not just because it was a childhood that I didn't appreciate back in those days, but also because it was spent in the place called Mexico. And to console myself still further (consolation and desolation sweep over me like great tidal waves) I borrow José Emilio's final sentence 'Who could feel nostalgic about all that horror?' Only there is a question mark in my version.

63

I've always been amazed at how close I feel to abandoned children, and I've never really been able to explain it properly to myself. Sometimes I think it must simply be due to one of the houses in which I lived as a child, the one on Niño Perdido (Lost Child) Street, number 13. Sometimes I think it's because of the colour of my hair, that is black or dark brown, while my sisters are blonde. I didn't have light coloured eyes either, and my sister Susana has blue eyes, and all my sisters use butter soap to keep their hair colour. I had curly hair like a sheep, which is why I've always felt a bond with black sheep. I've lost count of the times I've heard

My sister's wedding, 1961

my sister yelling at me that I wasn't my parents' real daughter, and she was always claiming she would throw me out with the garbage, but a lot of children must have heard similar threats, and felt much the same feelings. No doubt there's a Freudian explanation for it all.

The need to find an explanation for where I came from got worse the week I went with my daughter Renata to see *Remi*, a Japanese potboiler made for western audiences. It produced a great commotion in Renata who most certainly is a legitimate child.

My mother tried to help and told me the story of a Jewish lady 'half poet, half actress, who was very rich and whose husband lived in Veracruz.' This lady had no children and lived by the sea, which made her feel rather melancholy even though she didn't quite understand why. When my sister Shulamis was born she asked my mother if she would give her the baby (I think she must have intuited the secret wish of my sister Susana, who was just a little bit older). 'That lady tried to suggest that we didn't have enough money and that she could bring her up more freely,' says my mother, smiling. I smile too, but I watch her carefully and ask her what time I was born, but she can't remember whether it was six o'clock in the morning or six o'clock in the afternoon, so that I've never been able to have my horoscope properly told. That might help me get rid of my worry once and for all.

Someone once said that maybe it's all part of the feeling of belonging to the chosen people or that terrible sense of desolation that came over me on 6 January when I got out of bed and didn't find a single toy like the ones that the Catholic children were showing off down by the great tree. Nor did I seriously think of comparing myself to the Christ child when I saw him sitting on an altar in Tacuba convent or when I kept him close inside my soul or when I was out walking with the Lechuga sisters and Chonita in a procession. None of the Hanuka presents, not even the real silver coins that my uncle Guidale gave us when we went to see him in his bakery in Uruguay Street, were ever enough to rid me of that feeling of being an abandoned child, the feeling I've had ever since and which has driven me obsessively to read *Pedro Paramo*.

Maybe telling these family stories will help me understand it better. Maybe it can all be traced to the time when my father brought Susana a Shirley Temple doll back from the United States, dressed in white and orange silk pyjamas with a little embroidered dragon. I was so jealous I left home (which was then close to Argentina Street), and in those days I had a pair of apricot-coloured bloomers, and the boys all shouted, 'It's an old woman in bloomers,' and I had a rucksack in shiny blue material, which I took to school every day and which was all ink-stained, because we had to use those archaic inkwells. The real betrayal was the fact that nobody ever realized I'd run away at all.

64

I was a Zionist once. During the best years of my life, which I spent in San Ildefonso near José Clemente Orozco's frescoes, which made such an impression on me that sometimes when I look in a mirror and see myself haggard and over-made-up I seem to be the incarnation of some of those wretched women that the great one-armed artist painted. And that disturbing impression must have stayed fixed in my mind since the heavenly times I spent with my friends in the corridors of Number 1 Junior School. Or maybe it dates from the biology lessons at El Generalito school where they separated the boys from the girls to teach us about the mysteries of sex. This was also when we would be taken to look at the museum of unknown diseases, opposite the statue of Juarez, who in those days used to be wrapped in a fascist cape.

We came out as stunned as Malcolm Lowry was when he went to a museum of venereal diseases in Paradise Street. To try and recover from the experience we went for ice-creams to the Holanda in Guatemala Street or the café in the Parthenon which was run by a Greek who made excellent Greek coffee. The ice-creams at Holanda were Italian and were absolutely delicious. There weren't any Burger Kings then, but they did sell cider on the corner of Palma and 16th September Street, where we could also get hot dogs and something to drink while we listened to the barrel organ playing popular songs. One of those songs, 'A sign of absence' seemed like the best song in the world to me, as did 'Lost love' sung by Maria Luisa Landin. That was the time when I really got to know the José Maria Lafragua collection well, which was in a little walled off corner in the National Library in the Uruguay district, in an old Augustinian convent that kept having to endure all sorts of alterations. The best students used to work there, because Don Arturo Arnaiz y Freg — may he rest in peace! — chose them to help him update his huge filing cabinets and index cards. We used to spread out great sheets of marvellous handwriting, signed by the people who had put their names to the Apatzingan constitution or the many decrees of freedom written by the people who revolted against His Serene Highness. Thanks to Don Arturo, we learned a great deal about bedrooms and anterooms. The singer Agustin Lara was generally the favourite poet of my schoolmates — who were as sentimental as they were stupid. All sorts of important people used to walk round the great patios, including the new President's son and other aspiring parliamentarians. There was tall young woman with huge black eyes who was called the Senator, because her father was one and that was the time when Mexico started building supermarkets and freeways.

Actually, I was a dyed-in-the-wool Zionist and I made up my mind to go and work on the land in Cuautitlan, but my parents rescued me from the mud and my utopian ideas and forced me to go back to school at El Generalito. I would periodically escape to the Regis cinema to see films that were strictly forbidden, such as Gérard Philippe's *Le diable au corps*. He was my first and only love.

65

Ever since I went to see *Gone with the Wind* I realized that the cinema is a disaster zone. I've seen it twice: once, when my younger sister was really young, that is when she was five and for some inexplicable reason I was looking after her (maybe my mother was working, which is why I can so readily identify with the children who sell Kleenex and chewing-gum in the streets), and just when Scarlett O'Hara was about to turn her velvet curtains into an elegant red dress, my sister Shulamis said she thought the film was really 'boring' and I had to leave the cinema because people started getting upset, just like the time when my sister Lilly had had to leave a cinema with me. The next time I saw *Gone with the Wind* was on TV. It went on for two days and I can't remember all the variations in the plot because I got them mixed up with the ads.

One disaster I remember vividly occurred on a family outing to a film by Frank Capra with Carole Lombard and Don Ameche. We were sitting on the front row because my mother is short-sighted and didn't want to wear her glasses, and I was given instructions to read the subtitles out loud, even though I needed glasses as well but my mother wouldn't buy me any because she was afraid that I might think they made me ugly. Well, contrary to both my parents' expectations the other people in the cinema refused to tolerate my reading aloud and decided not to let us see the happy ending. Later, in New York, I went to see a Bergman film, and got into the cinema just in time to see Ingrid Thulin cut the most delectable parts of her anatomy with a piece of Baccarat crystal. I've never been able to set aside my duties as a babysitter, so I wasn't able to discover exactly how she managed to perform the operation. During another Bergman film, *The Source*, my father was stroking my right hand to help ward off the evil eye and at the crucial moment I shrieked: 'Oh God, she's being raped!' and the whole cinema shouted in unison, 'Shut up, you stupid cow!' and a low voice added, 'Is the girl pregnant?' and I said, 'No, they've just killed her. It's me that's pregnant.'

These unexpected events didn't prevent my father from being a devoted participant in film festivals all round the world, including the one that our own city bestows on us twice a year. He was so keen on attending that once they awarded him a medal of honour at the film festival because he had brought glory upon the event by his inimitable presence ever since the time when *La dolce vita* came out. Glory is not a constant thing, certainly, and the next year my father broke four ribs going up the stairs at the International Festival during the screening of a film called *Without Anaesthetic*. Even though he wanted to see the rest of the film, he was rushed to the English Hospital right in the middle of the excitement.

66

Jewish men cry a lot and Jewish women even more. In the days when I used to cry regularly I used to wonder why I never discovered the cause of so much dampness. Once, in a time of great crisis in Paris when I was pretty much out of touch with myself, I started re-reading Dostoievsky's *The Idiot*. I discovered that I had a bit of both aspects of the central character in me: the idiotic and the Russian. Elena Poniatowska says the same thing happened to her, and that she feels there's a strong Russian streak in her even though she's Polish, because when she goes to someone's house and sees a Ming vase (metaphorically speaking) she says, just like Prince Mishkin: 'I must take care not to break that, it's so beautiful, it belongs to my hosts and they're my friends and goodness knows where they got it from, and then I somehow edge over to it and break it.' In that instant we really come together, me the Jew, the Russian, the Mexican actually from Jesus Maria Street and her, the Pole, the personification of love, the Mexican with a Russian great-grandmother, Elena Irinov. I'm a secret Catholic and she's a secret princess, because she resembles Dostoievsky's marvellous prince. I identify more with Raskolnikov, who was working class, a pickpocket turned public speaker, someone whose very special way of speaking is something I feel close to. Just as all we Jews feel close to the proverb about onions buried in the ground, since onions make you cry and even soil can't stop that weeping welling up and overflowing and the skin peeling off in layers.

Why this meander? Well, it's just a tearful reflection on all the tears shed throughout my life (and my parents' lives). But tears are useful as a finishing touch. A few days ago I went to an engagement celebration for a young man in our family, my nephew David. My father was a witness in front of the reformist rabbi who was reading in Sephardic Hebrew, the Hebrew they use in Israel, and then he translated it into Spanish, explaining it all and removing all sense of mystery.

My father was the only one to maintain a sense of mystery: he went back to the table with tears in his eyes, tears which soon turned into a deluge, undoubtedly out of respect for the Great Flood, and of course out of respect for the brimming eyes of my mother, my sisters, my brothers-in-law, my cousins and even me.

I ask why. Everybody has a different explanation, my father is remembering his own sisters who died when they were young, without ever having been able to take part in the weddings of their own children and grandchildren, like he has. The rest of us are crying because it's contagious, because we feel some ancestral sadness, because we're really all just old onions.

67

Many years ago we lived in Tacuba, in three different houses. The first was a tiny house with a little garden, one of many like it in Claveria, which was a dusty area near the Mexico-Tacuba highway called the Gulf of Campeche. We had a dog, The General, a guard dog who was poisoned in accordance with a tradition that started many years ago in Mexico. Another rather hairy dog was pink, because my sister Susana had washed it in mercury; it didn't die, it just spent the rest of its life looking like Edith Piaf.

The next house was in Popotla, facing the Arbol de la Noche Triste, the night I always associate with the Popotla cinema, and also with some skulls that my father placed in the entrance to our adobe house and which turned out to

Mother, Lilly and I, 1932

have belonged to a young native woman aged about twenty and one of Cortes's defeated soldiers, who had neither a horse nor a helmet.

I used to sit down and cry every night when my parents went out and I was left with my sister Lilly who used to make me play freefall wrestling with her. We each had a fighting name, she was the Lion and I was the Tiger. By the end of the fight I was always the one on the ground and my sister used to threaten me with the skulls if I said anything to our parents. She wasn't naturally sadistic, she had become that way thanks to a maid we had called Paula, who used to make her take boiling hot baths without saying a word and spanked her if she didn't. I used to be made to pay for it later. We had a small shoe shop then where we sold black patent shoes for little old ladies and vampish shoes in grey or navy blue with very high heels and lots of buttons and bows for 23.50 pesos. Later on we had another shoe shop called La Nueva, which had the very latest city styles and Tacuba prices.

Around that time I saw *Dracula* too, and ever since then I've dreamed about him. Right now I'm writing a book about blood which starts with the tse-tse fly. Paula or some other

maid like her used to make me go to bed and walk down a
dark corridor, and I used to imagine the Transylvanian
count was lurking in the shadows. My parents weren't
around because Berta Singerman had arrived, or because
they were out having a coffee in the Principal.

That was also the time when I gave up the religion of my
ancestors. Lilly and I were learning English with some nice
ladies who had fallen on hard times and who lived with
their mother in an attic in the house next to ours. These
young ladies felt sorry for us, since we looked so angelic and
they were afraid we might die and miss out on Heaven: they
converted us to Christianity. We were baptized by a priest
wearing a coffee-coloured robe. He was from Popotla church
and his hands were covered with wild black hair. He blessed
us with a beaming smile and gave us his hairy right paw to
kiss. Ever since then I've not only dreamed about Dracula,
I've also dreamed about King Kong, to whom I dedicated my
book about hair. After our baptism we took our first
Communion, which was organized by the Sodi Pallares
family who lived in the village of Santa Maria la Ribera, in a
purple house with all sorts of ornamentation and Tiffany
lampshades. For our First Communion breakfast we had
tamales, atole, books and white leather missals with a
pretty gold crucifix on them. We used to go to confession
every Sunday and take communion and then go on to the
Popotla cinema to see the next instalment of *Flash Gordon*.
That's why my Christianity is mixed up with comic strip
heroes and characters from serials, including the Shadow,
Fabiola, Dracula and King Kong. It's definitely a marvellous
sort of Christianity.

68

Like the houses of the zodiac, the houses of memory are full
of mystery. I've just come back from a visit to 44 Jesus Maria

Street where I was born. There was a plastic curtain in the doorway: metres and metres of oilskin cloth on the table, and little covers in imitation crochet all over the place. Inside it looked shabby and rather decadent, outside the paint was peeling and an old ornamental stone crest on the front of the house was about to fall to bits. The staircase had long since gone, but when my parents lived there there were five lovely big rooms, a gigantic kitchen, a bathroom and an inner courtyard with about forty flowerpots. My mother rented out two rooms and lived in the other three rooms of the house with my father, Lilly, me and my uncle Volodia, who we loved like a father, sometimes more than our own father. Certainly we paid more attention to him. He had been sent over from Russia by my grandparents to look after his sister in 1928.

The Merced quarter is fascinating, starting with the old names that serve as reminders of the city's history: La Corregidora, Soledad, Mesones, Regina, where the first brothels were set up after the Conquest. The emigrants all lived there, in old colonial houses with high roofs and large courtyards full of flowers, wheeling barrows selling socks, bread, yellow soap and neckties. The local people were very kind and hospitable and always helped us a lot, and La Merced had a market rather like the one in Tacuba, where we also lived once, with no water and with just one room for all four daughters. The beggars used to stop by the shoe shop every Saturday with their tin cans, and we used to put in a centavo. Later in the week the beggars would come into the shop with their Saturday earnings and buy new shoes. We used to have to wrap their feet in the tissue paper of the shoe boxes, use a metal shoehorn and measure them for the latest styles, all the while our faces were turned away, after which we'd ask whether the shoe fitted nicely, the question we asked all our customers, including the ones buying little white baby boots, the sort that get dipped in metal and placed proudly on dashboards in taxis. Since there wasn't any water supply, it used to be sold in the street and on

Saturday we used to go to the public baths, in homage to those public bath houses where my father once went, the ones inhabited by demons.

The water was odd, sometimes it rained cats and dogs and flooded the shops, and we used to pay fifty centavos a ride to be carried on an Indian's back. When I tell this story I feel I'm a reincarnation of one of those characters that Riva Palacio painted so badly, but what I am certain of, regardless of where I was or which of the houses we were living in, is that those floods happened, and we had to use canoes to get about and there were Indian bearers too. I even remember my sister Susana playing with the street kids and saving rats from sewers.

In those days the market at Tacuba was like the one in Juchitan. The comedian Cantinflas had a booth near our house and his partner Chilinsky's wife, Tamara, used to visit my mother. She was very good-looking, blonde and nice. They never talked to Chilinsky, nor to Cantinflas, but when I remember him I make connections between the skulls of the Noche Triste, the hairy priest of Popotla, those latest shoe styles, the lack of water and the fiestas of Twelfth Night, when the local children were all given toys and we Jewish girls always wanted some too, and were always disappointed, even though were were pseudo-Christians.

My religious activities came to an end when my mother was bathing Susana one day (she must have been about four years old) and found a little medallion under her blouse. Lilly and Susana got a good hiding. My speedy trip through Christianity has left me with a decided preference for reading, and a fascination with torture. Every Sunday I used to think about Baby Jesus sitting on my heart and whenever I ate crunchy cakes I'd feel very uneasy, because I used to worry that it might disturb Him.

Probably the name that would have suited me best when I was a child was Rosita rather than Margarita; that's where my parents went wrong. Margaritas, or rather daisies, are white with yellow centres and lots of petals. I remember some photos which show me sitting beside other girls in my family, (my cousins Lila and Haya, my sister Lilly, Miriam, the new bride's niece) when my uncle Volodia married my aunt Celia. When she died in childbirth my uncle married my aunt Raya, who was very beautiful and wore a yellow dress, and had her hair in waves rippling over her forehead and my uncle looks very handsome in the photo, while I look gauche, my round cheeks like apples. My cheeks were so pink that my mother used to think I was running a fever, and sometimes she was right, so she would give me castor oil and hold my nose. Sometimes I'd be cold and there was a Hindu gentleman, a friend of my parents called Mr Bezra who called me Rosita and brought me chocolates. There was another one too, a Mr Baisboim, a bachelor who wrote poetry and who we all liked a lot; he used to call me *katchele*, duckling, because I've always walked rather like a duck, and then there was another poet, Meier Perkis, who was also a bachelor and called me *eretz Israel epele*, which means apple of Israel because of my brightly coloured cheeks.

Later, when I was older, I started to do my hair in the way I wanted, that is in a Pre-Raphaelite style, though that was completely beyond the pale in my teenage years, because nostalgia was not yet fashionable. Then I had another hair-style which might have been very radical if I had done my hair like that just before the Vietnam war or if I'd invented the rock opera *Hair* instead of some American gringo.

That's been my destiny, to always choose hair-styles that come into fashion later on, though when they did I was already completely out of date, and friends used to admire the way I looked like a Gustav Klimt picture, or an art deco model or a photo from the twenties by one of those men who made Coco Chanel famous. Now whenever I see pictures of the Tutankamun exhibition in New York or I remember my trip to Cairo, a long time before Tutankamun travelled round the world, I recognize what it means to look like a Pharaoh, or rather like a Pharaoh from the Lower Nile.

When I was a child my fortune was told by the flowers from Xochimilco, and those flowers often spelled out the name of Lupita, followed by Margarita. The whole family got together and we would eat reformed Jewish food and the adults would drink beer. Sometimes we would go to my uncle's house (the one who was a baker) who had only one grown up son, Oscar, and we all used to fight about him. That was on my father's side, on my mother's side there were two cousins, Elias and Micky, but we didn't see them very often. Whenever we went round to the bakery in Uruguay Street, my uncle would stroke my hair and call me Margarita, the name my family still calls me, which is in my passport and on my fortnightly pay cheques.

The sound of my name appealed to the insect world, and we used to have to perform disinfecting ceremonies to kill off the bedbugs. The house would be covered in paper and we would go somewhere else and sleep on the floor, while the poisonous fumes would attack the insects in the house we'd just left. The bedbugs sometimes used to climb out and run and get into the feather mattresses on the beds. My mother and the maid would take everything outside in the sun and air, the mattresses and quilts, and pour boiling water over them to kill off the bugs. Her vampire-like behaviour used to affect me and my sisters and we can remember with distaste the strong, unpleasant smell on those days. That was the time when the Nazis were starting to use the ovens in their crematoriums.

Every interior male journey has its opposite, that is, there is also an external female journey. I've undertaken this sort of journey in recent months, and by exploring the nooks and crannies of reality and the countries I've visited, I find myself seeking out my own origins, especially when strange coincidences happen. Those sort of coincidences are the reason why I love science fiction so much, and romantic adventure stories, even though they may be formulated in terms of invasions and end with frightening uncertainties that promise to hold you in suspense until next week's episode: more crunchy cakes, a few sweets, some popcorn and all the marvels of those adventures that are full of coincidences and never come to an end.

In three months I've met more people whose blood is linked to mine than ever came over to this virgin land throughout the ages, because all my ancestors are buried in Eastern Europe, or maybe in Germany, and sin is an amazing thing and we're all somehow related to the Czar and to Lenin. My cousin Sam Glantz came two months ago. He is the youngest son of a brother from the Glantz dynasty that emigrated to Philadelphia, and by a marvellous coincidence he has an eleven-year-old daughter called Margo, and I find my name repeated almost exactly in another language, though with a slight foreign accent. And there I am with a double, like those everlasting cabalistic twins. 'We are Schwester Kinder,' says my cousin Polina from Odessa, in between her sobs, yes, Sam and I (and Sam and Lilly and Susana and Shulamis) are all children of the same blood-line, siblings in speech and appearance, and through our veins there run some of the characteristics of great-grandfather Motl or grandfather Osher or grandmother Sheine. We spend several days peering at each other, looking closely at the shape of a nose or the colour of a moustache, and our relatedness emerges in the way we smile or the sort of food our mothers and aunts used to cook. But blood gives out other signals too, as it flows sleepily along our veins until it gushes out into our hearts, which beat rather faster than usual. We are friends, but we aren't brothers, because the truth is that there is a price to pay for brotherhood, and sometimes it's best to keep brothers at a distance, as the biblical story of Cain and Abel so clearly illustrates.

Still, even though I've met Miriam and Doris too, Sam's sisters, they made very little impression on me. Miriam used to have a big nose and was very slim, and though she still has the same nose it seems shorter now because the rest of her body has filled out. I remember that Miriam was always smoothing down the pleats in her skirt (pleats pressed in with a flat-iron) and I remember Doris whose blonde hair, straight as ears of wheat, was cut in a simple page boy style, like any ordinary girl from Central Europe. They didn't look like the young Jewish girls who used to live there, those girls with dark skin and light green eyes, (like my little niece Alla) and dark, curly hair, who used to be seen in the streets of Moscow and Leningrad and who were instantly recognizable. Sometimes they were confused with women from the Caucasus, but that's irrelevant. The real Russian and Polish women, and the Germans too are all blonde like my cousin Doris or like Susana my sister, or like Ilana, the daughter of my other sister, Shulamis.

Blood can give out all sorts of signals, blood circulates and when its instincts are roused then most likely you're dealing with a relative. That's certainly the case without exception in soap operas, but it doesn't work with Sam; blood has changed its course. Sam is primarily a friend and the voice of the blood-line is not very effective over the phone that connects me one day with my cousin Oscar, elder brother of Miriam, Sam and Doris, now a professor of sociology in Brooklyn. Oscar didn't have time to see me in the high pressure world of subways and skyscrapers, and all I remember of my cousin is a typical American voice, full of doubts and affirmations, scattered conveniently through our conversation which was very short. Oscar is named after my grandfather Osher, but I'm sure that if my grandfather had ever gone to New York or Philadelphia the same thing would have happened to him as happened to that character of Bashevis Singer: a shoemaker who came to the United States when he was about eighty, after his wife died, when all his children had been in the United States for years, making designer shoes. Well, that shoemaker got off the boat and saw with amazement some ladies and gentlemen who looked like Polish nobility greeting him with exaggerated gestures of cheerfulness. That's how my foreign uncles perceived my mother when she went to Philadelphia in 1945, while Susana was in a hospital bed in Rochester after they operated on her bad leg, the left leg (which had always hurt her when she were small, and which always ached whenever we knocked her left hand or her right ear). My uncles were waiting for the train from Minnesota, expecting to see a lady dressed like a redskin or an Aztec even though she was a Russian Jew just like the rest of them. That's what happens with relations and family histories. Blood flows and flows across continents, and the melting pot renders it down. All this is leading up to how I recently met Sam and his wife, who seem more like good friends than blood relatives. The problem might be due to the fact that we don't quite fit the requirements of the typical Jewish phrase 'we're children of the same sister' (because you get your Jewishness through your mother) since Sam is the son of my father's brother, Moishe Itzjok, alias Morris Glantz, a pharmaceutical chemist in Philadelphia. The old proverb may well apply in the case of Izy, only son of my uncle Leie (the uncle whom my father complained about because of his false kisses). Izy died of leukaemia in Philadelphia and when I think about him I remember three visits (which seem to have followed on from one another in my mind, but which actually happened over a very long period) of his to Mexico. His refined face and his light eyes, his shortness and his curly hair, his

MARGO GLANTZ

pleasant personality all combine to shape an image of him
and make him an important figure in a story, even though
we didn't share that story, first because he was so much
older than the rest of us, and secondly because we lived in
such distant, far-removed lands.

71

A little while ago I was talking about the kind of
coincidences that happen in soap operas. I was talking
about them because whenever you hope such coincidences
are going to happen they never do, that's fate, but when they
do decide to happen, nothing can get in the way. Let's take
an example: in this conscious and confused search for roots
(a marvellous dream) I set off for Eastern Europe, cradle of
my ancestors on both my father's side and my mother's. I
went to Russia so as to be the first member of my (Mexican)
family to retrace the journey my parents had undertaken
back in 1925 before they set off for Mexico, when they
left their motherland forever. My Mediterranean side came
to the fore and my siblings all looked at me and told me
how brave I was. To go on such an adventure in unknown
lands is always the distinguishing mark of an explorer and,
as I've said before, I am another Columbus, with my
grandfather Osher and my grandfather Mikail serving as
navigators.

My first encounter with the homeland was Kiev. I arrived
there from Budapest and landed on Russian soil, where a
guide was waiting for me with a shiny black car made in the
USSR. I was very moved by the journey across the plains
near the Dneiper, my heart beat faster and my eyes gazed
out in every direction over those steppes that were
impressed into my father's memory, but when I got to the
hotel a woman who looked just like one of those round
Russian dolls told me that I hadn't seen steppes at all, that

you had to go down to the southern Ukraine to see anything like that. I didn't see them, but I did meet several fellow Mexican travellers during a long day of guided visits to monasteries with golden domes shaped like onions, inside which were marvellous icons and frescoes. Afterwards we went to the catacombs, called *laura* in Russian, which were also full of icons and coffins, all intricately carved and containing mummified bodies of hermits who rather conquettishly were still wearing embroidered velvet slippers which sometimes even had little bits of mirror fastened in.

When we came out of the *laura* an additional person had attached himself to the Mexican contingent: a professor from the university of Kiev who taught Spanish, and whose protegée had been the professor of our young guide Olga, a girl wearing glasses and an antique coral necklace that her grandmother had given her.

He was a man about seventy, not very tall, fairly slim, with grey hair and melancholy eyes who spoke perfect Mexican Spanish. That evening he came to the hotel where some of the tourists gave him Mexican books, and he had read Mariano Azuela, Revueltas and Elena Poniatowska. We see him standing in the doorway. He asks me: 'Are you a Jew?'

That word Jew is so strong it almost seems like a command, if you say Jewish it's less violent.

'Yes, I'm Jewish. Are you?'

'I am too. I lived in Mexico from the age of twelve. I went over there with my parents and my sister in 1924 and stayed there until 1932, the year we went back to the USSR, because my mother missed her native country so badly. It was a very cold, hungry year. Later on there was the Great War of Liberation. In 1924 we were on our way to the United States, but we couldn't get there because they refused us entry visas. We went to Cuba, but since everybody else was going on to Mexico we went there too.'

'That's extraordinary! It's exactly what happened to my parents. Which ship did you sail on?'

'A Dutch ship, the *Spaardam*.'

The soap opera has come true! It's the very same ship! The same adventures, the same medical examinations, one member of the family about to stay behind in the city of Riga because he can't see very well in one eye and has a patch on one lung, meeting the ship brotherhood, those photos with the same well-known poses!

There's one thing though that doesn't match: the dates. The gentleman facing me travelled in 1924 with his family, whereas my parents went over in 1925.

'Ask your father if he ever knew my family. My father was a very refined man, very well-read, very gentle. He had always been fond of books. In Mexico he worked for the Soviet Embassy.'

Maybe he worked there in Kollontai's time, and maybe he'd used those huge abacuses, the ones with the beads that look like amber which they still use in shops and restaurants in Moscow, Leningrad, Odessa and Kiev. At the embassy, where my mother saw the ambassadress always ready to go out riding with Diego Rivera. The *Spaardam* went backwards and forwards regularly, always the same ship, the only thing that ever changed was the passengers and the cargo, the ship's master was the same, striding over the deck giving orders to the passengers or dining with them and ready to hand over the same entry fee for Mexico in dollars and explain about the two hundred dollars required as the open sesame for Veracruz. Yasha Perelman loves the USSR, once he studied at the conservatory and played the piano, but the war came, the Great War of Liberation as they all call it so proudly, and he was sent to the front, and afterwards he began teaching Spanish to enable young guides to show us round the *lauras*.

'I can remember a lot about Mexico City. We used to live right in the centre. I even had a girlfriend there.'

I'm in Acapulco, thinking about Perelman, in his native Kiev full of poplars and chestnut trees on the banks of the Dnieper. I'm sitting on some rocks on the beach at La

Condesa in Acapulco, huge seaweed covered slippery rocks
('Be careful, it's slippery,' says an American to me, and I
answer 'Yes' and go on staring out to sea). Some sunburned
boatmen go past, their hair bleached in the sea air, and try to
persuade me to take a boat out to the island. I don't answer,
a sort of sputnik goes threateningly past my head. I've just
finished reading Truman Capote's *Music for Chameleons*,
an investigation of cheating at cards that quotes Mark
Twain on the wickedness of mankind a lot, when two blond
boys go by, looking very suntanned. ('Skol? Coconut oil?')
The sea is bathing me, as it is them and filling the
Pepsicolas they're drinking with foam, they laugh, they're
nice looking, wearing red swimsuits and one has real
goggles, motorcycling goggles, their bodies are magnificent,
they laugh again, the sea goes on bathing me, leaving a salty
taste in my mouth and sand in my eyes and swimsuit. I feel
part of the ocean, I'm in the beginning of all things, I sink
into the sea and the waves lap at my muscles. The sea
reaches the rocks and I remember Perelman remembering
Mexico and Mexican songs and the old streets where his
girlfriend used to live. In the streets down by Guatemala? or
the Corregidora? It doesn't really matter, he went there in
1929 or 1930, he can't remember who the President was
then, he's thinking about his girlfriend or about Agustin
Lara, the singer. He asks me if I like the song 'Rosa' and I say
yes. He listens to it often, he says, his apartment is a very
small one, he lives with his Ukrainian wife who doesn't
understand any Spanish, he's very fond of her, and he loves
his son too and his one grandchild, but he still likes to
decorate the walls with reminders of Mexico, with things
like a huge Mexican hat, and he has albums of Mexican
songs, Maria Greever, Guty Cardenas 'who died in a bar-
room brawl when I was in Mexico.'

Yesterday I went into a jewellers in La Costera — La
Costera, with its filthy sand and exposed pipes and acres of
cars — just like our own town in fact. I saw something I
liked, a very unusual ring with a shiny cluster of stones. I

went in and asked the price:

'A hundred and fifty dollars.'

'Dollars? Don't you sell things in Mexican money?'

'Even Mexicans think in dollars these days, that's why we do it.'

There are two completely different Mexicos, and this is totally unlike the one Perelman means when he says:

'When the Bolshoi Ballet came to Mexico the first time they asked my advice about the sort of music they could use. I taught them "Las mananitas" and "Las golondrinas", and later they told me that people liked that a lot. I do miss Mexico, and when I feel totally homesick I put on the record player and listen to some of Agustin Lara's songs, I get my map out and I use my fingers to travel round.'

In Moscow I talk to Carlos Laguna, who has been in charge of the Embassy shops for the past fourteen years. I tell him my story while we eat caviar and mushrooms and drink vodka in the Arkanguelsky gardens, near the beautiful church with its violently coloured twisted domes, a miniature version of St Basil's Cathedral.

'Is it Perelman?' he asks.

'Do you know him?'

'Of course I do, he's always interested in news from Mexico.'

Then we go into the church, which is full of old ladies around seventy or eighty, dressed in black with head-scarves tied under their chins. There is only one man, who is also very old. They say their prayers, kneel down, kiss the ground and the icons, and there are flowers everywhere. We go out again and on to Peredielniko, where we visit Pasternak's grave. Beside him both his wives are buried. Some young people are there too, and the grave is covered with flowers. Russians love flowers, they are always carrying bunches of gladioli or carnations around, and brides lay flowers on the graves of unknown soldiers who died during the Great War of Liberation, our guide says very solemnly.

Back in Mexico I tell them what happened. My parents can't remember any Perelman family. On Saturday or Sunday we're all together at the table and I'm telling my story again to the rest of the family when my father suddenly gets excited and stammers: 'Perelman? . . . Perelman? Of course I remember! *er iz geven a guter Id* (He was a good Jew). Don't you remember, Lucia? You don't? I do, he used to have a magnificent moustache.'

My sense of nostalgia grows and grows, keeping up with my new friend, in fact it isn't nostalgia, it's melancholia, sweet, sticky and rose pink, like the song that Lara sang in the 1930s, when a Russian Jew was a young man of seventeen, chasing girls in La Lagunilla, back in the days when he missed the northern snows.

72

Once I start talking about coincidences, there's a lot more to tell. I think about the Jews crowded into the ghettoes in Odessa, and I see them as Babel saw them, all aspiring to live until they were a hundred and twenty years old, sitting along the low walls of the Jewish cemetery (which has long since vanished) and gazing out over the graves of all those people named in epitaphs. Sometimes I like to think about them, because my family doesn't have any heroic episodes in its past, it just has a few hiccups, like what happened to my brother-in-law when he was arrested as he got off an aeroplane in the United States, because his name was Jacob Guzik, and the people reading the blacklist thought they were dealing with the famous gangster by the name of Jake Guzik, the man who had been holding to ransom both the police and the underworld in Chicago, in much the same way as Leibl the King had held to ransom the Jews and the local police in the Moldavanka quarter of Odessa when the Czar was still in power. The customs officials realized that they had been misled and that they had got the wrong man, that my little, bearded relative was not the equally little but very dangerous Chicago gangster. They let him through, and here am I, writing about it all.

Sometimes I write down the conversations that my mother used to have with her friends, during recreation in high school, all those neighbourhood girls from Molda-vanka, and although they didn't talk about Leibl the King, they did talk about Mishka Yaponetz, Japanese Mishka, whose gang lived in the same area.

'Yes, Deribasovskaia was a very high class street, and so was the street I lived in, but Moldavanka was very poor, there were even beggars there, and sometimes there were "blind" ones who weren't really blind and who used to wrap their feet in rags when they went out begging, and then they'd mug people and work as pickpockets, just like used to happen in Tempito, where you went with your father to buy shoes. I was amazed when I heard that things like that were actually going on in Odessa, which my friends all knew about, though I was actually pleased later on when they told me that those same members of Mishka Yaponetz's gang had fought against the cossacks in 1919 or 1920 (that was the time of the pogroms in our area). Those cossacks were white Russians, they were killers and rapists. The gang killed them because they'd been burying people alive and beating and torturing. Hitler could have learned a few lessons from them. Mishka and his gang crushed them, they wiped them out and then went back into the ghetto and disguised themselves and put on bloodstained bandages as though they'd actually been victims.'

As I'm writing, Renata comes into my study in a rage and says:

'Mother, the only fun in this house is the sound of that typewriter.'

I tell Cristina this, and she suggests that I try to sell that statement to Olivetti, the makers, to help pay the cost of going to a psychiatrist in an effort to try and reconcile my daughter either to life or to her mother. I think it's enough for the sea to go on lapping at our feet, as is happening at this very minute. I also prefer to save my money, as I climb the steps opposite the sea that calmed Potemkin, the Chornoe More, the Black Sea, with my nephew Petia. He has green eyes and lives with his parents in a room in my hotel.

Later still I am walking down an arcade filled with baroque statues and crystal ceilings with another relative that I have only just met, and am learning more about the world. I cross the street, escorted by my two companions who are both engineers (everyone in the Soviet Union today seems to be an engineer; the same thing used to happen here in Mexico when everybody had a degree, including the tram drivers and community workers). They show me round the city and take me to the nicest places: the opera house, the Voronsov Palace, Pushkin's house, Red Army Street with all its cakeshops and the parks full of old ladies selling flowers, the museum, an old merchant's house, Deribasovskaia Street, which still retains its old Czarist name, like Peter Street, who was important 'because the revolution thought of him as a good governor', as a guide told me yesterday. Deribasovskaia, I learn, is named after General De Rivas, a Spaniard who fought against Napoleon.

'Yes,' says mother interrupting my account of the places I'd visited, 'I went there once as far as the Nikolaievsky Boulevard, I don't know what they call it nowadays, and I was just passing Count Voronsov's Palace, the one who was jealous of Pushkin. You must know where I mean, it's near the sea, and I heard shouting so I went up the staircase and into an enormous room full of antique furniture, Louis XV style, gilded furniture, not like the imitation things they make today but genuine antique Louis XV furniture, and I saw some young boys sitting round a bonfire in the middle of the polished floor singing and passing bottles round, and I felt really upset because it didn't seem right for them to be destroying such lovely things, it was pure vandalism. Now they really look after things in the Soviet Union, they have a lot of museums. Russians were always very honourable people, but in those days things were very difficult and the government was always changing and you didn't know what was going on from one day to the next. I was very young and my brother Salomon was a civil servant, he was in charge of removing furniture from a palace that belonged to one of the Rothschild's friends, and he gave the furniture to people who had once been servants in the palace and let them do whatever they liked with it, because he had no idea where it was all going to end and if anything would be saved at all.'

'That furniture might even have ended up in the National Museum where I went with Petia.'

'Yes, that sort of thing did happen. They liked me at school, they used to hug me a lot and try to get me to join the Young Communists and break away from my bourgeois past, but when they saw that I wasn't very interested they stopped being quite so nice to me. I remember once I was with a friend who lived in the apartment below us. A young man came up, one of our friends, wearing a uniform and carrying a pistol. He really thought he was something special, and I asked him since he had a gun if he knew how to fire it, and he took it out and actually grazed my skin with a bullet. I never did tell my mother about that.'

The statue facing the steps in Odessa is a statue of the great lord Richelieu, a relative of the famous cardinal, who lived in the city for many years, but the street once named after him is now named after Lenin. My father lived nearby, by the opera house, but that street is still called Richelieuvskaia. I went there with my guides, Petia and Zaik, reliving the image of my father as a young man, a bright-eyed youth wearing a striped cashmere suit and a matching Spanish-style waistcoat (just like the one my elder daughter Alina wears nowadays), a watch-chain hanging from his left pocket with a star of David (that pocket reminds me of other pockets, also on the left, in waistcoats draped over the end of the bed, when my parents were asleep and I used to hunt for coins which consoled me in school time, since I used to eat cakes during recreation periods in those miserable secondary school years) and fancy shoes, which can't be described in any other way, because they look like the sort of thing Clyde (of Bonnie and Clyde) or some godfather figure would have worn (two-colour shoes, in coffee and white) and that's my father, a godfather in the truest sense of the word, a great father, like the one in the photo, framed in purple velvet and silver given as a wedding anniversary present to my sister Susana:

'There you are, Susana,' says my father, 'a fatherly present.'

73

Locks of hair are sometimes put into lockets along with photos, and are worn next to the skin, where they stay nice and warm. Lockets are a sort of funerary urn for memories, and now I go back over old photos, place them in some kind of order, line them up and try to read new stories into them, while my friend Tono draws my attention to the studio photos, all carefully posed and constructed, even down to the clothes that had to be worn on the grand occasion of the picture taking. The click immortalized them all, as it immortalized my father, who has just appeared in the last story dressed as a godfather, with two-tone shoes, Mexican style trousers, a hand placed napoleonically over one of his front buttons, a flower in his button-hole, a smile on his lips and pride in his eyes, one arm resting on the shoulder of a much older man, one Yud Yud Schwartz, a Jewish poet who would later commit the sacrilegious act of translating the Old Testament into a profane language, that is, into Yiddish, a dialect turned language. That Old Testament written to be read as Holy Scripture, handed down by Moses to the Jews when God prevented them from entering the

Promised Land. Right now that Promised Land is causing us all sorts of problems.

Now it's my turn to be in a photo, and there is my mother too, offering me a dice so that I will keep quiet for the camera which demands absolute silence and immobility and I'm not looking at the dice, I'm looking at the camera, as is my young mother, in a white dress with black spots and a white collar, her hair smoothly brushed and a slight smile round her mouth, like the Mona Lisa, and I'm looking startled and Lilly sitting on a high chair is also staring with fascination into the camera.

There's another photo where mother appears with Lilly going up an imaginary staircase; behind them is the vague patterning of a wall hung with old tapestries, very art nouveau, but all as fake as the staircase beside them. Lilly is dressed like a little pre-war English girl, with a little fur hat and a mackintosh and my mother is wrapped in a fur coat that hangs languidly and elegantly from her shoulders. My father appears in it too, looking older and leaning against a pedestal that looks like an exaggerated prop from an opera. Susana is sitting down on her own, wearing a rather strange outfit, that is, a suit with a hood and you can tell that it's all handwoven and blue because it tones with her eyes which are most certainly blue and there's a little hat on the top of her head. She is sitting on a bench and even though she is so small, her pose seems to be the most carefully studied of all.

The only one of us who was never photographed in a studio is Shulamis, and photos of her very obviously date from another moment in time, when pictures were more homely, more natural and were usually taken at home when grander families owned their own cameras (they used to go shopping in the United States or buy them on the black market in Mexico) and captured all their children's special moments instantaneously. Of course there is a photo of Shulamis taken in a studio, with my father who looks old now. Her hair is wild and uncombed and hanging down in red strands all over the place. That photo is signed by one of those photographers who has a booth in Argentina or Chile Street where my parents were photographed at a still later date. There are other photos too, the kind taken in parks with a big camera on a tripod and a bellows like a large accordion and we're all dressed up as Mexican cowboys or wearing wreaths of flowers round our heads, sitting in one of those flower-decked shallow boats called *chinampas*.

There is also a very special photo, one that you can hardly see because the paper on which it is printed is so old and yellowed and sepia-coloured, that was taken of me with a group in the San Martin Park in Buenos Aires. Two of the people in that picture are dead, and the other is as good as dead in my life (how strange the way things turn out!) and the one whose finger pressed the button to take the photo, an old Polish man, had emigrated like my parents to America, sometime before 1910, before the Great War. He was Polish, not Jewish and he talked to us rather sadly, like someone watching it start to rain, about his family that he had left behind waiting for him in some Polish village while he set off for America, and he had tried hard, saving carefully, saving as carefully as he could to pay for a modest passage in that Wagnerian ship. We are now in 1969.

74

I continue in Acapulco. I look down at myself and my eyes take time to focus, as happens often on the beach when the sea changes all the colours of everything around you. The mirror reflects a triple image back at me, my profile reminds me of a Roman emperor's. It startles me, in the same way I was startled when I first discovered my profile at the age of sixteen. Luckily, I tell myself, this profile looks like that of an emperor and not like a slave thrown to the lions, but I don't move yet, I'm riveted to the spot, thinking as the image of the emperor Nerva floats through my mind, the

Father and the family

one whose head was cut off and remodelled and placed on the body of the emperor Diocletian, and I prefer to have the profile of any ordinary Christian who got thrown to the lions and preached at by Paul, the Jew.

I go out with Renata, and I look at my somewhat fat body and feel a sense of regret. A mature woman, which is the kindest way to describe her, goes past, incredibly fat in a purple bikini, with her flesh hanging out shamelessly round the sides, escorted by a man whose chest droops worse than mine does. I feel consoled. I go down to the beach. It's getting dark. The sea lightens memories and stirs breezes. On the beach they are still selling shrimps and marinated fish, battered fish, necklaces, dresses, earrings, piña coladas, and I feel at one with the sand and the spray (in a kind of salsa rhythm) while I mentally go back over the story of my family tree, I revise it all, it's time to bring things to an end, if not completely then at least for the time being. I reflect on reaching my half century with the same precise, peaceful astonishment and with the same wild, archaeological enthusiasm that Napoleon must have felt when he saw the Pyramids on his way through Egypt . . .

Coyoacan, Odessa, Acapulco, Leningrad, Warwick
1902? — September 1979 — October 1981 — August 1986 — June 1989.

Glossary

Amor, Pita (1918–). Mexican poet.

Akhmatova, Anna (1889–1966). Real name, Gorenko. Russian poet and translator. Joined Acmeist movement in 1912, but, following death of her husband at hands of Cheka in 1921, Soviet publishers refused her work. Condemned for aestheticism by Communist Party in 1946, only to be rehabilitated seven years later.

Azuela, Mariano (1873–1952). Pseudonym, Beleno. Mexican physician and writer. Doctor with Francisco ('Pancho') Villa's army during Mexican revolution, and later director public education Jalisco province. Leading chronicler of twentieth-century Mexican politics, with over twenty novels. Principal work: *The Underdogs*, written in El Paso, Texas, in 1915. Recipient national prize for literature in 1949.

Bauer, Felice Fiancée of Franz Kafka.

Bieli, Andrei Russian symbolist poet.

Carrillo, Lilia (d. 1974). Mexican painter. Exponent of a revived surrealism, by way of reaction to abstract art.

Carvajal, Juan (1932–). Mexican writer.

Coronel, Pedro (1922–late 70s). Mexican painter and sculptor. Great colourist, and artist of depth and force.

Cuesta, Jorge Mexican poet. Member in the 1930s of the contemporaneos, associated with the magazine, *Contemporaneos*, which led the revival of Mexican lyric poetry.

Delgado, Rafael (1853–1914). Mexican writer. Realistic novelist, published in the 1890s and early 1900s.

Diaz Miron, Salvador (1858–1928). Mexican poet and political journalist. Aspired to hold political office, but his campaign ended, more than once, with incarceration for attempted murder.

Felguerez, Manuela (1928–). Mexican painter and

sculptor. Exponent of a revived surrealism, by way of reaction to abstract art.

Garcia Guerrero, Luis (1920–). Mexican painter.

Garcia Ponce, Juan (1932–). Mexican writer, literary critic, and editor.

Gongora, Leonel. Colombian painter. Lived in Mexico in 1960s.

Gonzalez Martinez, Enrique (1871–1952). Mexican poet. Poet, physician and political secretary until 1911, later Mexico's ambassador to Spain, Argentina and Chile. Long considered critic of modernism, but now seen as Mexico's leading modernist poet.

Jacob, Max (1876–1944). French poet. Linked to surrealists. Killed by Germans.

Kollontai, Alexandra (1872–1952). Pseudonym, Domontovich. Government and party official in Soviet Russia. Revolutionary from 1890s, later Bolshevik. Various government posts, and later head women's department of Communist Party. Soviet diplomat from 1922, mainly in Norway. Accredited to Mexico in 1926, and recipient of Mexican honour. Author of books on women's movement, and articles and pamphlets on sexuality.

Lara, Agustin (1897–1970). Mexican composer of light music. Famous from 1930, establishing world-wide reputation. Also sang own songs.

Leivik, E. [? Leivick, Halper (1888–1962). Yiddish writer. Born in Russia, died in New York.]

Marin, Lupe (d. 1983). Second wife of Diego Rivera.

Opatoshu, Joseph (1886–1954). Yiddish writer of novels and short stories. Born in Russia, died in New York.

Orozco, José Clemente (1883–1949). Mexican painter. A founder of the muralist movement. First Mexican to paint mural in the United States, and often contrasted with Rivera. Considered by some a leading twentieth-century painter. Mainly murals in Mexico.

Pacheco, José Emilio (1939–). Mexican writer, and sometime university lecturer abroad. One of Mexico's leading poets. Also wrote novels and short stories. Winner national poetry prize in 1969.

Pilniak, Boris (1894–1937). Real name, Vogay. Russian writer. Took no part in revolution, and travelled abroad. Published stories and novels, mainly in 1920s. Arrested by state security, and died in prison. Later rehabilitated.

Pitol, Sergio (1933–). Mexican writer of fiction.

Poniatowska, Elena (1933–). Mexican writer. Well-known journalist and author of works of fiction and non-fiction. Principal works: *Dear Diego*, a reconstruction of Angelica Beloff's letters to Rivera, and *Massacre in Mexico*, about the 1968 student riots.

Prieto, Luis (1929–). Mexican oral historian. Director of the Centre for the Study of the Mexican Revolution.

Quiroga, Rosita (d. 1985). Argentinian singer.

Revueltas, José (1914–76). Mexican writer of novels and short stories from a revolutionary perspective. Awarded national literary prize for *El Luto Humano* (1943), but *Los Errores* (1964) considered major work.

Riva Palacio y Guerrero, General Vicente (1832–96). Mexican statesman and novelist. Helped establish Mexican short story. Historical fiction, influenced by Dumas and Manzoni, greatly popular in his day. Principal work: *Cuentos del General* (1896).

Rosas, Ignacio (d. 1950s). Mexican painter. Muralist.

Shklovsky, Victor (1893–1984). Russian writer and critic. Principal theoretician of formalist movement, and close to futurists in literature. Joined socialist revolutionary party in 1917, and later forced to flee country temporarily. Principal work: *Sentimental Journey* (1923). Formalism proclaimed dangerous in 1929, later engaged in literary history and dramatic and film criticism.

Urrutia, Elena (1932–). Mexican journalist.

Zeifulina [Seyfullina, Lidiya] (1889–1954). Russian writer. Member socialist revolutionary party, 1917–19. Experience of revolution in provinces led her to write short stories and other prose. Recognized mainly in 1920s.